EMBERS

THE PHOENIX PROPHECY
BOOK FOUR

CARA CLARE

ARCANE

THE PHOENIX PROPHECY SERIES

Book One: Nova
Book Two: Blaze
Book Three: Ashes
Book Four: Embers
Book Five: Flames
Book Six: Fire Bird
Book Seven: Blood
Book Eight: Ice
Book Nine: Snow

Prequel novella: Hollow

Books 1-6 can be read as a complete story arc.
Books 7-9 follow Nova and the guys as they face a new threat.

When above turns to darkness
And below breaks free
A witch born to humans
Salvation shall bring
Fated to five who are not what they seem
The Phoenix will rise and become Earth's Queen
Into the embers
One
Two
Three
Devoured by Flame
The Phoenix is She

TANNER

Water wraps itself around my limbs. It's cold and dark beneath the surface of the lake, and quiet. The jittery, fractured sensations in my head disappear when I'm down here. I need to come up for breath —I've been under for too long—but I don't want to feel the harsh night air in my lungs. I don't want reality to come rushing back.

Since the second jump, when I hopped into Sam's head and found him in *Spine*, I've been struggling to hold it together. The guys know it. Nova suspects it. But I keep on telling them I'm okay. I'm good. I'll be fine.

Am I fine? No. I'm not.

Having Sam close doesn't help. Sometimes, when he's near me, it's almost impossible to keep his emotions out of my head. Like, because I was inside him, the wall between us is more fragile than the wall between me and the others.

Sometimes, letting myself feel what he's feeling is intoxicating. Like when he touched Nova for the first time, and when he was inside her for the first time. Then... well, fuck, it was incredible. But other times, even when he looks okay on the outside, a darkness scratches at his core. We've all survived a lot of bad shit, but Sam's story is worse. Much worse.

Physically, emotionally, Sam has spent his whole life in pain. Nova's presence is healing him, but the pain is still there. Perhaps that's why he reminds me of myself. A distant version of myself. The way I was when Kole and the others first found me.

My chest is tight now. About to burst. I push my arms down by my sides and torpedo back up to the light. When I reach the surface, I flick my head back and send an arc of water into the lake. The droplets glimmer in the moonlight.

Kole is waiting for me on the jetty. His long, thick legs are dangling over the side. His boots are next to him, feet in the water. It's an oddly casual pose; he spends most of his time brooding with his arms folded.

When he sees me, he draws his legs back and pulls on his socks. "Don't know how you're still alive after swimming in there. It's freezing," he says, offering me a hand and pulling me up beside him.

Standing with my crotch at the level of his chin, I shake my arms, purposefully spraying him with water. His eyes flicker a little as he appreciates my wet torso. But then he stands too and says, "It's time. Nearly midnight."

I pick up my towel and rub it over my hair and face. The moon is bright, but clouds are coming in. That's good; we'll need its cover once we're out of the woods.

"Sure you want to do this?" I ask, wrapping the towel around my waist as we head back to the cabin.

"We need to know what's going on in town." Kole unfastens his hair and lets it hang loose over his shoulders. He fiddles with the band, slides it onto his wrist, then reties his hair again. "And something's not right about this..." He stops and looks up. When the light touches it, the mask we cast over the cabin quivers like water.

"You think the Bureau should have found us by now?" I ask him.

"They made a show of scouring the woods, but they stopped before they got anywhere near the mask." He lowers his voice as we approach the cabin. "Plus, a spell this powerful? They should be able to detect its energy. The fact they're not trying to break through means something else is going on."

"Mack agrees?" I pad up the steps toward the veranda.

Kole nods. "And Luther. They're worried the Bureau *wants* us here. Out of the way."

"Why would they—"

"I don't know." Kole opens the door and steps aside for me to walk through it. "Hopefully going back into Phoenix Falls will answer that question."

* * *

INSIDE, we change into dark pants and sweatshirts. Nova watches us from the bed. She's wearing a forest green sweater that makes her eyes look tantalizingly bright. She bites her lower lip, looks as if she's about to say something, then decides not to.

Walking over to her, Kole slips his hand to the back of her neck. His thumb brushes the bruise his teeth left on her skin. Their eyes meet. A wave of lust hits me. It's radiating from them like heat from the sun. I watch as Kole dips his head and kisses her. Slowly, deeply, like he wants her to remember every second of it.

Arousal settles in my core. I clear my throat and they look round at me. "As much as I wish we had time for a goodbye party," I say, putting my hands into my pockets, "we need to be in town by three a.m. if we want to make the most of the quiet hours before sunrise."

Kole nods, pinches Nova's earlobe lightly between his thumb and forefinger, then heads for the stairs. "Meet you outside," he says to me before he disappears.

"You're sure we don't have time for a goodbye party?" Nova opens her legs and I slot myself between them. She hooks them around the backs of my knees, nudging me closer.

Sweeping her hair from her shoulders, I kiss her forehead. "You have no idea how much I wish we did."

She laughs and raises her eyebrows, glancing down at the slight bulge in my pants.

"Okay, maybe you do have an idea." I pull her to her feet, wrap my arms around her waist, and kiss the spot where her jaw becomes her throat. When I look at her, my chest tightens. "I love you. You know that, right?"

Nova frowns and lifts her arms up, looping her hands behind my neck. "Of course, I do." She rests her head on my chest. "You'll be back soon."

"We'll be back soon." I breathe in her scent as I hold her close.

We stay like that for a moment. Her heartbeat merges with mine. I don't want to leave her. Everything in my body is telling me not to leave her, but the voice she heard hasn't told us to stay put. So, I'm assuming we're doing the right thing.

Downstairs, Sam and Luther are playing cards, but Mack is nowhere to be seen.

"Snow needed to blow off some steam," Luther says. "He's been cooped up for too long. You're all set?"

"All set." I glance at the door. Kole's bulky frame is outside waiting for me.

"Head for Rev's. Ask her what's been going on. Watch and

learn only. You need to be in and out of Phoenix Falls before sunrise." Luther fixes his eyes on mine. "Right?"

"Right." I pat his shoulder. "Don't worry. We'll be fine."

Something I don't sense very often from Luther fills the air around him. He's genuinely scared for us.

"We'll be fine," I repeat. "And hopefully, by the time we're back, you'll have had some luck on the research front."

Slightly guiltily, Nova and Sam look at each other, then at the discarded laptop on the table. So far, their archive searches have resulted in sweet fuck all. But that doesn't mean they won't be lucky eventually. Right now, I'm praying to the moon they will be. Because if we're going to figure out how we're supposed to save the world, we need more to work with. A lot more.

"Good luck." Sam stands, leaving his hand of cards face up and causing Luther to release a frustrated growl. "We'll keep researching." He nods at me then hesitates. "When you see Sarah..." He stops, clearly unsure what he wants to say to the woman who both abandoned him and helped save him.

"I'll tell her you're doing good and that you'll see her soon." I pat his shoulder, smile, then ruffle his curly black hair. "See you soon."

I kiss Nova one more time before leaving. By the time I reach the door, Sam's arm is around her waist. Outside, I pause for a moment and inhale slowly. Waiting on the bottom step, Kole looks in my direction.

"They're a good fit." I trot down to join him. "Sam and Nova. It's happened fast, but he's one of us. You feel it too, right?"

Kole presses his lips together and makes an *mmm* sound. "Yeah, I feel it. Which means she almost has her five..."

"That's not a good thing?" I ask, trying to interpret his growl.

"Could be," he says. "Or it could be that the fifth guy tips the balance, triggers what's about to happen, sets things in motion..." He stops and shakes his head. "Or I could be talking bullshit."

"You're a seer. Shouldn't you know if you're talking bullshit?" I ask, raising my eyebrows playfully at him.

In another time and place, Kole might have reprimanded me for back-chatting him. I'd have let him, and one thing would have led to another. A flash of heat passes between us. But there isn't time. Not now.

As we start our journey through the trees, I glance back at the cabin. Soft orange lights glow from the windows. "The fifth has to be Luther. Doesn't it?"

Kole looks back at the cabin too. A strange expression crosses his face. "Perhaps."

"What does that look mean?" There's something he's not telling me.

He glances at me then flexes his fingers at his sides. Shoving a branch out of his way, he says, "Luther told me he can't stop thinking about her. Since the club. Apparently, *all* he can think about is her."

I pause, trying to figure out why Kole seems so pissed. "Okay, and that's a bad thing? Didn't you expect it? There's been a simmering, hate-you-but-want-to-fuck-you tension between the two of them ever since she arrived." I laugh a little and push my fingers through my hair. "And after the club? They were at *Spine* together. They slept in a hotel room. In the same bed—"

"I get it," Kole snaps at me. He inhales deeply then repeats, a little more calmly, "I get it, but Luther's not exactly known for treating women right."

"You're worried his intentions aren't as pure as yours?" I deliberately hold Kole's gaze. He rubs the back of his neck; he knows I'm talking about the biting. About the fact that, just because it's making him superhero strong instead of psycho-killer strong, we all seem to suddenly be okay with him drawing blood from her.

"That's not fair, Tanner. It's different. We share a blood bond. We're—"

I hold up my hands. "I get it." I nudge his elbow with mine. "All I'm saying is that every single one of us is drawn to her, and we all have our own issues to contend with. Luther's history with humans is complicated. So, maybe he's struggling to make that fit with how he feels about Nova."

"She's not human."

"Anymore," I say firmly. "She's not human anymore. But she was. She was raised human in a town full of A.M.A. zealots. You can't blame Luther for being confused."

A low growl comes from Kole's throat. Usually, it's me and Luther getting on each other's nerves, not Kole and Luther—those two have been brothers since the Academy.

"Do you know how Nova feels about him?" I ask, pushing leaves out of my face as the forest thickens.

"Do *you*?" Kole replies.

I shake my head. "I haven't asked."

"But you must sense something when she's around him."

"She feels so much when she's around us these days, it's hard to tell who's making her feel what." A proud sort of chuckle ripples my chest. She feels a lot of stuff. A lot of *good* stuff. "Maybe just let them figure it out, Kole. Luther knows that if he hurts her, we'll kick his ass."

Kole glances at me, then releases an unexpected laugh. "'Fraid I did more than *kick* his ass."

I keep walking but grab his arm. "You and Luther?" My eyes widen. Immediately, my cock pays attention. "No way?! When?"

"Couple of days ago."

I tilt my head to the side. "Did you tell Nova?"

"She was surprised, but okay with it."

9

"Of course, she was," I laugh. "Who wouldn't be okay with that visual?"

Kole's about to reply when he stops walking. He raises his palm. In front of him, the mask shimmers. We stop talking. "Ready?" he asks me, taking a step closer.

Reluctantly, I push the image of Kole and Luther from my head. "Ready."

2

NOVA

K ole and Tanner have been gone less than five minutes when Snow finally ambles back up the cabin's steps. He can barely fit through the front door, and Luther yells at him to be careful as he stomps dirt across the living room.

Sam watches carefully as Snow shifts into Mack. "It's different," he says, cocking his head. "We keep our clothes. Werewolves, I mean."

"Shame," I tell him, enjoying the flush of color in his cheeks.

"They've gone?" Mack asks, standing stark naked in the middle of the room.

I nod, appreciating his exposed body and the fact he's never even been a little bit embarrassed to be naked in front of other people.

Looking at Luther, he says, "I'll change, then we'll talk. I have an idea."

Luther frowns in response but he doesn't move from the couch—just takes a long sip from his whiskey glass. "Sounds ominous," he says.

Instead of replying, Mack turns and strides toward the stairs. I watch him for another long moment then, finally, I take my gaze away from his perfect butt and tell Sam I'm going to sit outside for a while.

"Need to clear my head before we..." I gesture to the 'research' table.

"I'll join you in a minute," Sam replies, squeezing my waist.

On the veranda, I sit down and cross my legs. It's cold out, and my sweater isn't thick enough to keep me warm. I raise my palm, blink at it, and a ball of flames appears. Conjuring fire from nowhere has become easy. Second nature—or perhaps first nature. But as Professor Mack told me a while ago, I'll need more tricks than this to defeat what's coming.

I know that now, and it terrifies me.

Since all this started, one thing after another has taken my attention away from the fact that an ancient prophecy says *I'm* the one who is supposed to save humanity. Somehow, I'm supposed to stop this primal, evil force from being unleashed on the world. But no one seems sure precisely how or when I'll be expected to show up and save the day.

The guys keep telling me I'm powerful but, right now, they seem far more powerful than me.

Curling my fingers, I set the flames free, leaving them suspended in the air in front of me, and sigh as their warmth licks my face.

Watching the trees, I try to calculate how far Kole and Tanner have gotten by now. I hate the fact they've left. I hate the fact they're going back into town when we know bad things are happening there. But I know it's necessary; we need to know more, and we need to know fast.

After a few quiet minutes, Sam joins me. He's holding two

steaming mugs. Passing me one, his eyes distracted by the floating fire ball in front of me, he says, "Hot chocolate."

I smile and breathe in the smell of the cocoa.

"Your mom used to make us hot chocolate." He sits down next to me. "When we couldn't sleep or if one of us had a nightmare, she'd make hot chocolate and put those funny little sprinkles on the top."

"In the shape of a smile," I add, the memory tugging at my chest. "I remember."

For a moment, the two of us sit side by side looking out at the lake and the trees. Then I ask Sam, "Is it strange? That Kole and Tanner are going to be seeing Sarah?"

Sam presses his lips together, thinking about my question. "Yes," he says. "But I think I need a little more time before I come face-to-face with her." He shakes his head, his curly hair falling over his forehead. "It's been so long. I remember her, but..." He sighs. "I don't know, it's all a bit muddled in my head."

"There's no rush," I tell him. "She'll wait as long as you need her to."

Smiling at me, Sam sips his drink. Then he says, "How about you? Are you alright?"

"Fine." I'm not very convincing.

"You're worried about them?"

I breathe in deeply. Being apart from Kole still feels so wrong, so unnatural. My body fizzes with the need to be closer to him. Every second, I fight the urge to run after him. And Tanner? My heart can't handle the thought of something happening to him. But that's too much to put into words, so I just say, "We don't know what's happening in town. Last time Rev came out here, she told us people were behaving strangely. That bad things were going on."

"Bad things?"

"That's why the boys need to go. If it's got something to

do with Ragnor and what he's planning, we need to know." I uncross my legs and stretch them out in front of myself, rubbing my left thigh with my empty hand. "We also need to know what the Bureau is doing. If their agents are still looking for me or if they've given up and moved on."

Sam flicks his hair from his eyes. It's dark, and curly, and thick. "How about you?" I ask. "Are you alright?" I look down at my hands. "After last night…"

Laughing a little, Sam inches closer to me. "After last night," he says, "I'm very all right."

He meets my eyes and brushes a loose strand of hair from my face. "We didn't rush you?" I ask. Worry flutters in my chest; it felt right at the time. In the moment, making love to Sam felt like the most natural thing in the world, but it was his *first* time. "We kinda ganged up on you."

At that, Sam shakes his head. A crooked grin dimples his cheek. "You definitely didn't rush me, or gang up on me." He takes my mug, setting his and mine on the veranda behind us. "Nova, I spent eight years locked away. Feeling nothing but pain." He cocks his head. "And the occasional quick, dirty orgasm—alone in my cell."

I flinch at the word 'cell'. I haven't asked Sam what it was like to live and work at *Spine*. I want him to tell me when he feels ready. I don't want him to feel he owes me a story or an explanation of where he's been for the past twenty years.

"Last night, for the first time in my life, you made me feel like I was in control. The three of you gave me something incredible, and I won't ever forget it." He turns my hand over and kisses my palm.

"And you're not freaked out that we're…"

"That we were almost siblings?" Sam tilts his head from side to side. "For a long time when I thought of you, you were my sister. I used to rewrite the past in my head. Imagine the fire never happened, that I'd stayed with you, that Charles and Alice asked me to call them 'Mom' and 'Dad'." He breathes in deeply. The mention of the fire brings hot tears to the back of my eyes, but I blink them away. Sam is stroking my palm. "But maybe that's because I didn't know any better. Maybe the way I missed you, the way I longed for you… maybe it was always something else and I just couldn't recognize it." He lets go of my hand and shrugs a little. "Does that make any sense at all?"

I angle myself toward him and reach out, tracing the line of his jaw with my index finger. "Yes," I tell him, "it does." I'm about to slide my hand lower, over his chest, when I stop myself and sigh. "We should go inside." I jerk my head toward the door. "Research."

"I'd leave it a while if I were you," Sam says, glancing at the window. "Polar Daddy and Fire Daddy were having a pretty heated conversation." He chuckles at himself. "No pun intended."

In front of me, the flames I made spark higher. "Fucking Luther," I mutter.

"You guys don't get on?" Sam frowns at me. "I thought… *fated to five*? He's not one of your five?"

Tutting, I roll my eyes. "No, he isn't." As the heat in my belly subsides, I pick at a loose thread in the hem of my sweater. "Luther hates humans."

"You're not human anymore."

"Maybe not, but apparently any amount of human is too much for him." I bite the corner of my lip, remembering what Luther confessed to me in the darkness of our hotel room. "After the club, he told me some things about his past. I thought we were making progress." I sigh again and flex my fingers. "But since we got back, it's like he can't stand to look at me. Even worse than before."

"Probably because he can't stop thinking about you in

that outfit." Sam nudges me. When I look at him, his eyes are travelling across my chest.

"You remember that?" I fold my arms in front of my stomach, suddenly self-conscious.

Sam's eyebrows twitch. "Nova, I will *always* remember that outfit." He pauses then asks, "Did you bring it back with you?"

"Maybe." I meet his gaze. I know we should go back inside but, instead of getting up, I edge closer and swing my leg over him so I'm in his lap, my chest pressed up against his.

For a moment, Sam doesn't move. The juxtaposition between the way he looks—ridiculously handsome, confident, like he could devour me if he wanted to—and the nervous excitement in his touch when he gets close—like he can't believe he's allowed to touch me—is almost too much to handle.

His hands skim my sides and land on my waist.

"What do you want to do to me?" I ask, lowering my mouth to his ear.

Sam breathes out heavily. "So many things," he replies, nuzzling my neck in the exact spot Kole bit me.

Sitting back, I push my fingers through his hair. "You're in control now, Sam." I let my arms drop to my sides. "I'm yours."

As his cock twitches beneath me, Sam's eyes widen.

I slide my hands up beneath his shirt, the fire behind my back growing as I touch him. "They took too much from you," I tell him, meeting his eyes. "I know what that's like. I know what it's like to feel only pain, never pleasure."

His heartbeat quickens beneath my palms.

"It's your turn to take. Your turn to feel whatever you want to feel."

Sam's eyes dart past me toward the trees. "In the forest," he says. "I want to fuck you under the stars."

I stand up and give him my hand, pulling him to his feet.

I've put out the flames, and I'm about to head for the steps when he tells me to wait.

I turn to look at him. He puts his hands in his pockets and looks me up and down. "Take your clothes off."

A shiver runs up my spine. His tone has changed. It's deeper, more commanding.

He straightens his shoulders and repeats, "Take your clothes off."

Despite the fact it's freezing, I hook my fingers under the hem of my sweater and pull it over my head. My sneakers follow, then my socks, my pants, my tank top. When I'm in nothing but my bra and panties, I cross my arms. My flesh dimples with the cold.

"Don't hide from me," Sam says, taking a step closer. Then he gestures to my underwear. "These too. Take them off."

I swallow hard and do as I'm told.

My bra goes first. As soon as my breasts are exposed, the cold air stiffens my nipples into almost-painful peaks. Next, I remove my panties.

"Hands behind your back." Sam stares down at me. He's almost six feet tall, way taller than me. My core flutters as he licks his lips.

When I clasp my hands together and tuck them behind my back, my naked breasts jut out toward him. I'm utterly vulnerable. Every inch of me is on display. Sam reaches for me, puts his hands on my hips, and turns me around slowly. He hums gently into my ear as he leans in and runs his fingers over my body. He smooths his palms over my neck, shoulders, arms, and stomach. He examines every inch of me. He sinks to his knees and studies the swell of my thighs, kisses the backs of my knees, caresses the curve of my ass.

The moonlight hides some of my flaws, but not all of them.

When he reaches the tattoo on my thigh, he presses his thumb to it and looks up at me. Our eyes meet. Something passes between us. A shared whisper of a life. A shared understanding of what it is to be owned by another person.

Sam kisses Johnny's name. He swirls his tongue over my skin like he might be able to lick the ink clean from me. He runs his hands up the insides of my legs then, just when I think he's going to put his tongue to my core, he stands.

Taking my hand, he leads me down the steps into the trees. When we reach a spot where the moonlight breaks through the canopy above, he positions me beneath it. I wait for him to come to me, but he doesn't. He steps back.

"Show me how you make yourself come," he says hungrily. "I want to watch you."

My heart flips over in my chest. He wants to watch me? Right here? As he leans back against a thick tree trunk, his eyes sparkle. And suddenly, I get it. I'm the show. He's the audience. He's taking back his power.

"Can I sit down?" I ask, glancing at the forest floor.

Sam nods.

I lower myself to the ground, lean against the tree opposite him, and open my legs. The moon is a spotlight, illuminating me just for him.

Sam remains standing.

Closing my eyes, I slide my hand down my body.

"Look at me," Sam snaps. "I want you to look at me."

My cheeks flame red as I do what he says. I fix my eyes on his and begin to make slow circles around my clit. He studies my face, not taking his gaze from me for a second.

Finally, as I slide my finger inside myself, Sam walks over to me and crouches down. He takes hold of my wrist, jerks my finger out, then raises it to his lips. As he sucks the wetness from it, he closes his eyes and sighs.

I take the opportunity to reach for his belt. When I unfasten it, he snaps his eyes open. I pause. "Do you want me to?"

He hesitates for a second, then nods.

"Tell me." My fingers move slowly. "Tell me exactly what you want me to do."

"Take my pants off."

"Then what?" As I tug his pants over his hips, he sits back.

"My underwear."

I remove that too.

"Lie down." Sam watches as I settle onto my back beside him, then moves on top of me. Kneeling, he brings the tip of his shaft to my clit. I bite my lower lip. I expect him to plunge into me but, instead, he slides his tip up and down my folds. Arching over me, he lowers his mouth to my nipple. And then, as he takes my peak in his mouth, he thrusts. He fills me up. I wrap my legs around him. But then he's gone again. This time, he turns me over and pulls me up onto all fours. "Is this okay?" he asks, curling his arm around me.

"You're in charge," I tell him, inching back, dying for him to be back inside me.

Sam doesn't need telling twice. He digs his fingers into my hips and slams me onto him, and then he's like an animal. Like he wants to touch all of me all at once and doesn't have enough hands. He plays with my nipples, bites my shoulder, runs his hands up and down my back, then reaches for my clit.

Pleasure cascades through me as he moves his hips, finding new angles, and rhythms, and depths. I come hard, but he doesn't stop. I try to move his fingers, but he won't give in. He keeps touching me, brings the orgasm back, so it's both pleasurable and painful at the same time. A delicious torture that explodes in tiny fireworks all over my body.

"Will you swallow it?" he asks, his mouth next to my ear. "If I come in your mouth, will you swallow it for me?"

I'm panting, limp in his arms, trembling all over, but the trepidation in his voice makes me want to start all over again. "Only if you're a good boy and give it to me nicely." I smile at him over my shoulder.

Barely hesitating, Sam pulls away from me and stands up. I kneel in front of him and open my mouth.

"Don't suck, just hold it there," he says, hand on my chin.

I blink up at him as he rubs himself over my tongue.

"Fuck, Nova, your eyes." He stares down into my face. "You're incredible." Then his whole body tenses. He grabs the back of my head and thrusts his cock into my mouth. My eyes water. He holds my face, stroking my hair like he's trying to be rough and gentle at the same time, shooting thick ropes of cum to the back of my throat.

I look at him when I swallow it down, salty and hot.

Sam stares at me as if I'm a goddess. A smile breaks his lips, then he drops to his knees and kisses me, not seeming to care that he can taste himself in my mouth.

He cups my face, kisses my cheeks. "I'm sorry, was it—?"

"Don't apologize," I laugh. "I mean, I'm not going to do that every time but—"

Sam laughs too and wipes my lower lip with his thumb. "Nova," he whispers, then he smiles. "Little Star? Isn't that what the guys call you?"

Hearing my nickname on Sam's lips is a whole new level of dreamy.

"That's not enough," he says, shaking his head. "You're too bright, too strong, too fiery to be a Little Star." He kisses me again then pulls me into his arms. "You're everything." He holds me tight. "You're the sun."

3

KOLE

s soon as we reach the outskirts of town, it's obvious something is different here. Something washes over me. Darkness. It settles in my limbs and makes me feel ice cold. Tanner feels it too; his face is pale and he's rubbing his temples.

"What *is* that?" he asks, keeping to the shadows as we inch closer to the town sign.

"I don't know, but whatever it is, it's bad news." I glance at the sign. *Phoenix Falls—Where Ashes Turn to Light.* It's swaying gently even though there's no breeze.

"Straight to Rev's?" Tanner asks.

I nod, gesturing for him to follow me so that we loop round the back yards of the houses on Acacia Avenue instead of walking beneath the streetlamps.

As we draw nearer, Tanner looks longingly in the direction of the falls.

"You miss them?" I ask quietly.

He nods. "I miss the quiet," he says. "The lake helps, but there's something different about the falls. Something that soothes the ache, you know?"

My jaw tenses. I do know. But until Nova came along, I didn't. The only thing that soothed my ache—the hunger in my veins and the pain in my soul—was the brief moments of relief I had with Tanner. For me, Nova is water. Her fire pummels the darkness out of me the way the falls beat Tanner's pain from his limbs.

We're almost in the center of town when we hear shouting. At the back of The Cross, we wait in the trees and watch as three earth mages spill out onto the pavement. An air witch follows them. She's yelling, spinning a cyclone of autumn leaves into the air. It's impossible to tell what they're fighting about, but when roots start to protrude from the sidewalk and a tree nearby creaks angrily, I step in. Without revealing myself, I lock the roots back down, steady the tree, watch the three earth mages waver on their feet. Normally, something like this would take effort. With Nova's blood inside me, it's a cake walk.

As if the mist of rage has cleared, the pissed earth mages stare at one another then move off down the street with the air witch following behind.

"Who's running the bar?" Tanner asks as we press ourselves up against the side wall.

"Don't have time to find out." I jerk my head across the street. *Rev's Threads* is in darkness. For now, the street is empty. We run across the cobbles and dart down the alleyway to the back of the store. Instead of knocking on the door, I take out my cell and text Rev. *We're here. K & T.* There's a moment's silence before we hear movement inside. We wait patiently, then finally the door opens.

Rev ushers us into the darkness of the stairwell. She doesn't speak until we're upstairs in her sunshine yellow, dimly lit apartment. Then she pulls Tanner into a fierce hug and squeezes my hand. "You made it. You shouldn't have come," she says. "I'd have come to you."

"We needed to see for ourselves," Tanner tells her, stepping back and looking around the room. "Is Sarah here?"

Rev cants her head toward what I assume is a bedroom. "She's sleeping. I can wake her—"

"Not yet," I tell her, folding myself into a chair at her small round table. "First, let's talk about what the hell's going on around here."

Grimacing, Rev puts the kettle on the stove, opens a cupboard, and takes out three bulbous mugs made of hammered metal. She sighs and leans back on her countertop. "Can you feel it?" she asks. "The energy?"

Tanner and I exchange a knowing look. "We felt it," he says. "The second we entered the town."

"It's seeping into everything." Rev wrings her hands together in front of her stomach. "People are fighting, stealing, fucking. More than usual, I mean." She raises her eyebrows. "List any one of the seven deadly sins and, right now, Phoenix Falls is full to the brim with people enacting them."

"Tanya and Jake?" I ask, annoyance gurgling in my chest at the fact two inexperienced kids are now running the town instead of Mack and Luther.

Rev shakes her head. "They were told they'd get back up from the Bureau but, honestly, I can't figure out what's happening. All of the S.D.B agents seem to have cleared out. Reporters too."

"We noticed the news going quiet," Tanner says.

"It's like there's suddenly an embargo on even mentioning Nova." Rev takes the kettle off the heat as it starts to whistle. "Which should probably feel like good news, but—"

"I agree," I tell her. "It's not right. Something is off."

There's silence for a moment while Rev pours hot water into the mugs. She adds some questionable smelling teabags and hands us each a drink. "Chamomile and lemon balm," she says. "It's too late for caffeine."

"Smells great," Tanner tells her sarcastically.

Rolling her eyes at him, Rev takes a seat at the table. Tanner sits too, and we watch her expectantly. There's something on the tip of her tongue. I can sense it. Finally, she says, "So, what's the plan? How long are you going to hide in the woods?"

"Until we figure out what happens next." Tanner blows across his tea, takes a sip, and wrinkles his nose at it. "We know The League want Nova because they're trying to unleash some kind of big bad on the world. We just have no idea how they're planning to do that, or when, or where."

A strange look crosses Rev's face. She puts her mug down and laces her fingers together. "I might be able to help with the *where*," she says. When neither of us speaks, she adds, "Sarah and I did a tracing spell. We were trying to figure out where all this dark energy is coming from."

"I thought Sarah was unelemental," Tanner says.

"She can still do spells," Rev counters. "She has a wand, and she's quite powerful actually."

"Okay," I cut in, not in the mood for a debate. "And you found the source?"

Rev presses her lips together then breathes in heavily. "The Hollow," she says. "The dark energy is coming from The Hollow."

4

NICO

Hot vomit spills onto my shoes as I brace my hand against the wall of the house. Behind me, Eve is chanting. What she's chanting, I have no idea, but it sends shivers of nausea to my soul.

There's a dead body. A dead *woman* lying in an open coffin. A woman Ragnor hugged. A woman whose flesh hangs, decaying, from her pale bones.

I screw my eyes shut, trying to rid myself of the image that's burned into my brain.

When Mother finds me, she is so pale her skin is almost translucent. She lowers herself to the ground, sitting in the dirt, her back pressed against the cold gray stone behind her.

"Who is that?" My voice cracks as dry, frightened words leave my mouth.

Mother hangs her head and scrapes her fingers through her short, dark hair. "Elena," she whispers.

"Who the fuck is Elena?" I sit down next to her and draw my knees up under my chin. "Mom?" I turn to her, praying she sees that I *need* to know what's happening—that I can't be kept in the dark any longer. "Who is she?"

When she answers me, her words are barely a whisper. "She was Ragnor's wife." She glances at me. Her scar seems brighter than usual. "Ragnor and I were together. He was my alpha." She closes her eyes. "But he chose Elena over me. He fell in love with her, and he left me. Two months after he left, I discovered I was pregnant with you."

Cold shivers drip down my spine. I knew Ragnor left my mother. I never knew when, or why, or that it was for another woman.

"She was human." Mother looks up, stares over toward the fountain where Ragnor is still arched over a coffin. "She fell pregnant too, but she died after the baby was born."

"A baby?" I frown, my thoughts tripping over one another. I don't know whether I'm more shocked that Ragnor—the head of the Human Extinction League—was married to a human or that he got her pregnant. "I have—"

"A brother."

"A brother," I breathe.

Mother looks at me. "Sam."

Sam? That name… it can't be a coincidence? My mouth hangs open. I can't speak. Nothing will come out.

"Yes," Mother says. "The same Sam." She rubs the back of her neck and shakes her head. "Ragnor gave him up when he was a child. Sent him to foster care. He ended up with Nova's family but that was a long time ago, before we suspected who she was." She laughs a little. "Fate or a coincidence? I've never been able to decide."

"That's why I look like him? Nova's foster brother is *my* brother?" I stand up, my legs fizzing with the need to pace, to walk, to run. "Why didn't you tell me?" I round on her but when I see the dejection in her face, I crouch down and take her hands in mine. "Mom? Why didn't you tell me?"

Sniffing loudly, wiping her eyes with the back of her hand, my mother sighs. "Because Ragnor told me not to."

There is silence for a moment. We both know Ragnor is not someone you say no to.

She points a long, pale finger toward the coffin. "When Elena died, Ragnor got wrapped up in the dark magicks. He joined H.E.L. and worked his way through the ranks." She presses her lips together. She's physically shaking. "He made a pact."

I can barely hear her. I move closer. "What kind of pact? Is that what Eve was talking about? The Phoenix in exchange for…" A shudder ripples my shoulders. I know what I heard. *We give him the Phoenix. He brings your love back to you.* But my mind can't make sense of it.

Mother's lips twitch into a sorrowful smile. "That's what all this is about, Nico." She waves her hands in the air. "Ragnor promised the Shadow King he would find The Phoenix." She swallows hard. "He promised to give The Phoenix to the king, so that he may rise. In return…" She is staring at the coffin now. "The king will give Elena her life back."

"But he hasn't captured Nova. We failed. *I* failed." In the distance, Eve is now dancing barefoot around the coffin.

Mother takes my hand. "No, my love, you didn't fail." She squeezes it tight. "We know exactly where she is. Ragnor is just biding his time."

I swallow down a lump of fresh ice-cold fear.

"Nova and her boyfriends are hiding behind a mask in the forest outside of Phoenix Falls. They can't leave; the Bureau is looking for her. So, all Ragnor needs to do is open the portal and tell the king where she is." She nods at the coffin. Her gaze is dark and vacant. "Then Ragnor will have his wife back." She looks at me and lifts her hand to stroke my face. A silent tear rolls down her cheek, following the groove of her scar. "He'll have his wife back, and the world will crumble."

5

NOVA

Sam and I enter the cabin holding hands. Mack and Luther are standing either side of the kitchen, glowering at one another. They stop when they hear the door close behind us. I study them both. Mack is pissed, it's written all over his face. Luther is pissed, too. His skin is quite literally fuming.

"Did we interrupt something?" I ask, folding my arms and staring at them.

"No." Luther grabs his whiskey bottle from the countertop and pours another glass. He's drinking too much. Since we got back from *Spine*, he's had a whiskey in his hand more often than not. Catching me looking at him, he defiantly pours in a little more.

I glance at Sam. I'm not up for refereeing an argument. Not right now. "We promised Tanner and Kole we'd carry on researching." I gesture to the table and Luther's ancient laptop.

"It's pointless," Luther spits. "You won't find anything. Mack was just giving you kids a job to keep you out of the way."

"Luther..." Mack almost growls. "I don't know what's gotten into you lately, but you need to snap the hell out of it."

As they square up to each other, I let go of Sam's hand and march over to the kitchen. "Okay, I was going to let this go, but *you two* are the ones behaving like kids. What the fuck is going on?" I put my hands on my hips and wait for one of them to speak.

Mack gives in first, turning to me with a contrite expression on his face. "I suggested something Luther doesn't like. We'll fix it, Nova. Don't worry."

"What kind of something?" I'm not going to let him get away with not telling me.

"Go on." Luther raises his eyebrows. "Tell her your grand plan. See what she thinks." He takes a long sip from his glass. Heat is still coming off him in waves. It intensifies when he looks at me. Do I piss him off that much?

I widen my eyes at Mack. Sam has joined me and is leaning on the counter.

"I suggested we speak to Annalise in person," Mack says, hands in his pockets. "I don't believe she betrayed us. Either Tom ignored her orders, or he never spoke to her in the first place."

"Okay," I say, relaxing my stance a little. "And why do you think we need to speak to her?" Glancing at Sam, I quickly explain. "She's an old contact of Mack's from the Bureau. We thought she'd told the agents to stand down, but they attacked The Hollow anyway."

Sam nods. He turns to Mack. "You think she can help you?"

Sighing a little, Mack leans back on the counter opposite us. He rubs his beard as he says, slightly sheepishly, "Luther's right about the research. You won't find anything. We've looked at every archive, every book, every ancient text.

We've never found *anything* related to The Phoenix Prophecy."

Indignation tugs at my chest. He really did give us a fruitless task just to keep us busy?

Noticing the look on my face, Mack says, "I didn't want you out of the way. I wanted to keep your mind busy. That's all."

I soften as he fixes his gaze on mine. "Okay." I cock my head to the side. "But you think Annalise might know something? Wasn't she your boss when Kole first accessed the prophecy? If she knew anything about it, wouldn't she have told you then?"

"Honestly?" Mack shakes his head. "I don't know, but even if she can't help us figure out what Ragnor is planning, she *can* call off the agents." He turns back to Luther. "We need them off our backs, Luther. You know we do. We can't fight Ragnor when we're too busy fighting them. We can't even leave this hell-damned cabin while they're out there waiting for us. If Annalise—"

"I hear you," Luther says loudly. "But it's too dangerous. First of all, you've got to get close enough to speak to her. Second of all, you know jack-shit about her these days. It's been five years since you saw her. You don't know she'll even give you the time of day. You don't know it wasn't her who told Tom to do what he did." Turning to me, slamming his glass down on the counter, Luther continues, "Ask him *how* he's planning to get in front of Annalise." He jerks his thumb at Mack. "Go on. Ask him."

I chew the inside of my cheek. Flames bite at my insides. Luther is infuriating, but there's clearly something Mack isn't telling me. "Mack?" I wait for his answer.

Bracing his hands on the counter behind him, Mack exhales heavily. "We need to get you in front of Annalise. We need to show her your blood tests, and we need her to see you. Talk to you."

I nod slowly. "Right…"

"Every year, the Bureau holds a fundraising gala." His shoulders are tense. Hell, his entire body is tense. "It's tomorrow night. If we could—"

"If you could sneak Nova past an entire hotel full of agents who want to lock her up, everything will be rosy?" Luther scoffs. He picks up his glass again and waves it as he speaks. "You're supposed to be the big papa bear. The one who wants to protect her, and you're suggesting parading her in front of—"

"I *will* protect her." Mack practically roars his reply and launches across the kitchen.

Flames surge in Luther's glass-free hand.

Before he can throw them, I jump between them and hold out my arms. My own fire rushes from my palms, forming two walls of heat. "Stop!" I whirl around, staring at them. "Both of you."

Behind my fire, Mack stops and lifts up his hands.

Luther dampens his own flames and backs up.

"Do you realize what you're doing right now?" I clench my fists, and the fire disappears. "You're talking about me as if I'm not here. You're fighting about something that involves me, and neither of you have bothered to ask what *I* think. What I *want*." I stare up into Mack's face. "I know Luther can't stand me, but I thought you respected me more than that."

Mack's face crumples. He puts his hand on my arm. "Of course I respect you."

"Then ask me," I say defiantly. "Ask me what I think."

A soft smile appears on Mack's lips. "What do you think, Nova?"

Drawing my shoulders back, I nod at him. "I think we

should do it. If you know how we can get into the gala, we should do it."

As Mack squeezes my arm, Luther tosses his glass into the sink. "Fuck this." He throws his arms up, pushes past me, and storms outside. As the door clatters on its hinges, the place where Luther's body touched mine burns red-hot.

TANNER

"Y ou're sure?" I ask. "The Hollow? Could it just be because of the fight? All the magick we used battling the S.D.B. agents?"

Rev is about to reply when a door on the other side of the room creaks open. A gray-haired woman, perhaps in her sixties, steps out. She's tall and thin, wearing a thick beige cardigan on top of long white pajamas. "We're sure," she says, answering my question. "I don't know this place—The Hollow—but that is where the spell led us.

As if to prove it, Rev spins around and pulls a large town map from a drawer behind her. She spreads it onto the table. Sure enough, right where The Hollow sits, there's a big black mark. Scorched, like charcoal.

"Then I guess we're off to The Hollow," Kole says gruffly. He's standing up, leaving his barely touched mug of tea, when Sarah steps toward him.

"You're Nova's..." She searches for the word. "Friends?"

Kole folds his arms in front of his chest. Anger pulsates around him. Sarah betrayed Nova. She might have been doing it to save Sam, but she still betrayed our girl.

His anger merges with Sarah's guilt. It's nauseating. She's consumed by it.

"Kole." I put my hand on his arm and look at him in a way I hope says, *Don't be too hard on her.*

Turning back to Sarah, Kole says, "We are Nova's boyfriends."

Sarah doesn't seem surprised, just sucks in her cheeks then lets out a shaky sigh. "Please tell her I'm sorry for what I did."

"She knows." I step in and clasp Sarah's hands between mine. I can't stand here and let her feel this way; it's suffocating. "She knows you're sorry and she's forgiven you."

I sense Kole raising an eyebrow at me.

"Sam also sent a message." I tell her. "He said he's doing good, and that he'll see you soon. We just couldn't risk him coming with us tonight."

A million questions burn in Sarah's eyes but even if she asked them, we wouldn't know the answers. We don't know how Sam ended up being owned by *Spine's* Madame. We don't know the gritty details of his life there, and I'm not sure he wants us to know.

"We have to go now," I say, hugging her briefly. "We'll see you soon."

We're at the bottom of the stairs when I feel Sarah start to sob.

* * *

PROMISING Rev we'll be careful, we leave the center of town and make our way slowly toward The Hollow. Everywhere is now eerily quiet, wrapped in a stifling blanket of darkness. Even the stars are hard to see tonight, and the closer we get to The Hollow the more I feel like we should turn back.

Knives of ice are pricking my skin. Kole is so deathly quiet that I know he's feeling the same.

By the time we get there we're both breathless, but not from exertion—from the cloying heaviness in the air. Fear grips my insides. I stop and brace my hand on a nearby tree. Kole turns back. "Tanner?" His face is etched with concern.

I shudder. I'm shaking all over. "There's too much of it." I swallow hard and a sickening metallic taste fills my mouth. Not blood. Something else.

"Evil," Kole mutters. "Tastes like evil."

We don't even try to approach via the gates, instead heading straight for the trees. Remnants of the damage Kole did when he tore the trees' roots from the ground are evident in the rivets of upturned earth and fallen branches. Kole conjures a small green light and sends it ahead of us, so that if there is a barrier it will warn us.

We find nothing until we are at the tree line. With the lawn and the house in full view, the light bounces off an invisible shield. Not a mask, just a shield.

As we look out toward the fountain, my blood runs cold.

Eve, the witch who almost killed Kole, is standing on the rim of the fountain. She's barefoot. The lower half of her dress is sopping wet, and she's smiling up at the stars.

The jolt of fear that rushes through Kole's body makes me flinch. But then his features settle into something else... anger.

"They're here," he whispers. I follow his eyes and see a tall, dark-haired woman striding down the steps from what was our kitchen. She has a scar on her face, cropped hair, and she's wearing a short leather jacket. Nico is next to her. Side by side, they share something—a resemblance. "Kayla," Kole growls.

"That's her?" I narrow my eyes and stare at the woman Kole has told me about over a hundred times. The woman who haunted his nightmares for years after he left The League. I heard about her while I was their prisoner, but I never met her.

At the bottom of the steps, as Kayla shouts at Eve and asks what the fuck she's doing, Nico puts his hand on Kayla's arm. It's a strange gesture. Not one of a subordinate or a lover.

"He's her son," Kole breathes. "That traitorous little weasel is Kayla's son."

Looking at the two of them, it clicks. She is very clearly his mother. "What are they doing?" I ask, scanning the rest of the lawn. "Is that a coffin?" I tug Kole's arm and make him follow my gaze.

"Looks like one," he replies darkly.

We continue watching as Eve hops down from the fountain. She's too far away to hear, but she looks happy. Excited. With bouncing footsteps, she skips over to the coffin then bends over it as if she's talking to whatever the fuck is inside.

From the house, a group of werewolves in human form emerge. They're carrying a large wooden chest. They bring it to Eve and, when they open the lid, she plunges her hands inside.

She starts taking things out. White stones, a skull, feathers, crystals, and lastly a thick, leather-bound book.

"They're getting ready to perform a ritual," Kole says. I'm about to ask him what the hell kind of ritual involves an open coffin when movement catches my eye. A tall figure appears at the top of the steps. White-blond hair, slicked back over his thick skull. Long black coat. Tattoos on his knuckles.

He gazes down at Eve, then his eyes snap up. He tilts his head. He's looking right at us.

7

NOVA

"What do you remember about them?" I ask, propping myself up on my elbow.

Sam and I are playing cards upstairs on the bed, staying out of Mack and Luther's way. He has a terrible habit of exposing his hand, but this time places it face-down as he considers my question. "Your mom and dad?"

"They were yours too," I tell him.

Sam's nose twitches. "Not really." His thick curly hair falls into his face as he rubs the bed sheet between his thumb and forefinger. "I hoped they would be one day, but I don't think I earned the right to call them my parents."

"Earned the right?" My forehead creases into a frown. "That's a strange thing to say… you don't *earn* parents."

With a low-pitched chuckle, Sam says, "Maybe not. I guess what I mean is that it was my fault we lost them. So—"

"Your fault?" I sit bolt upright and don't care that my cards fall from my hand face-up.

"I bit you, Nova." Sam glances at my arm, even though there's no scar to look at. "We were playing. I bit you. That's why you started the fire." He meets my eyes. "They died because I hurt you."

Sliding over to him, I rub my hands over his broad shoulders. Beneath his shirt are the scars I find both hypnotizing and devastating at the same time. I can almost feel them through the fabric. I take a moment to find the right words. There are so many things Sam and I need to say to each other, it's hard to know where to begin. "When Kole unlocked my memories and showed me what I did, I thought guilt was going to swallow me up. It was like a dark shadow was squeezing the life out of me. I didn't know how I was going to live with it." Sam strokes his index finger up my arm as I talk. "But then I realized something."

He tilts his head and studies my face.

"I realized that we're part of something bigger. What happened to Mom and Dad was part of something bigger."

"The prophecy?" Sam's voice is low and thoughtful.

I nod, my hair falling over my shoulders. As it tickles my chest, I push it back and Sam's eyes catch on my tattoo.

Smoothing his palm over my chest, he examines the pattern. Five planets orbiting around a full moon, with intricate, swirling patterns stretching up toward my throat. "Tell me about this," he says softly, his fingers pausing their journey as they reach the raised flesh beneath the moon.

"My ex-boyfriend Johnny—"

"The guy in the video?"

"He was with the A.M.A. He branded me with their crest."

Sam's eyes snap to mine. They dance with anger. His jaw settles into a tight line.

"I asked Kole to cover it for me." I look down at my chest. "Apparently, seers are good at intuiting what people's tattoos should be."

"This is what he saw for you?" Sam moves closer and brushes his lips across my collar bone.

I'm leaning into the warmth of his mouth when we hear the door downstairs clatter near off its hinges. Leaving our cards face-up, we head quickly for the stairs.

In the living room below us, Tanner is bent double, breathing heavily. Next to him, Kole's chest moves quickly up and down. Below his tattoos, the veins in his neck are bulging.

Without speaking, Kole strides over to where Luther is sitting and snatches the whiskey bottle from him, taking a deep swig. Even though Tanner barely drinks anything but water, he takes the bottle from Kole and does the same.

Luther rises slowly from his chair, exchanging a worried look with Mack while Sam and I trot quietly downstairs to join them.

As Kole and Tanner stand side-by-side, passing the whiskey bottle between them, my eyes sweep their bodies for signs of a fight or an injury. Physically, they seem fine, but their faces tell a different story.

"Is Sarah all right?" Sam asks with trepidation.

"She's fine." Tanner answers quickly. "She and Rev are fine."

Striding to the couch and sitting down heavily, Kole says darkly, "But The Hollow isn't."

Mack waits for him to explain. If he's worried about his home, he doesn't show it.

"Ragnor is there. We saw him. With Eve, Kayla, Nico, and a bunch of werewolves." Kole grits his teeth as he speaks their names.

"Looking for Nova?" Mack asks.

Kole shakes his head. He pulls his hair loose, the way he always does when he's trying to release some tension from his body, and leans onto his thighs. "I don't think so." Kole looks for me and, without being asked, I go to him. He pulls me onto his lap and holds onto my waist as if he's trying to ground himself with my presence.

In a shaky voice, Tanner says, "There was a coffin. An altar. It looked like they were preparing for some kind of ritual. They sensed we were there. They didn't see us, but we had to run."

"A coffin?" Mack rubs his beard as if he's trying to put the pieces together but coming up blank.

"We couldn't get close enough to hear what they were saying, but there's something in the air." Tanner visibly shudders. "Evil, Mack. Pure evil."

"It's seeping through the town," Kole adds, his large Viking-like grasp tightening on my waist. "Making people behave strangely."

"Then this must be it," Mack mutters. "It's starting."

* * *

WE TALK for what feels like hours, going round in circles until we're so tied up and exhausted we can't think straight. Eventually, I tell them we should go to bed.

"We need to sleep." I run my hands up Tanner's arms. While Kole seems to have shrugged off the darkness they felt at The Hollow, Tanner is still sickened by it. "*You* need sleep," I tell him.

When he agrees, we leave Luther in the living room and go upstairs. There was a time when I hated sleeping with anyone else. With Johnny, I used to dread the nights he decided not to pass out on the couch and came crawling into bed with me. But with four burly mages curled around me, I feel safer and more loved than I've ever felt in my life.

My sad existence in Johnny's apartment in Ridgemore feels like it happened centuries ago and, even though I'm probably in more danger now than I've ever been, I would choose this life a million times over.

This life, and these men.

They all fall asleep before me. I like it that way. I try to keep my eyes open, so I can learn the lines and grooves on their faces, and the way their bodies feel against mine. But as my breathing slows, and warmth envelops me, sleep finally has its way with me.

When I wake, everyone else is still asleep. Kole's arm is across Tanner's waist, and my head is on Tanner's chest. Sam slept at the foot of the bed, hugging my legs, not yet comfortable enough with the other guys to be part of our night-time sandwich. Behind me, Mack is the big spoon. His strong arms encircle my waist. Wriggling back against him, I feel his morning erection stir in his pants. I look over my shoulder to see him open a sleepy eye and smile at me. "Nova," he whispers. "Go back to sleep. We've barely had a few hours."

I wriggle again but, when he refuses to play back, I stroke his face, kiss him, and say, "I'm going for some water. Don't move."

Sliding out of bed, I turn and look at them. The four of them. My heart swells. Not that long ago, I didn't think I'd find *one* man who would treat me the way they do, who'd make me feel the things they make me feel, let alone four.

I stop at the door and grab my long gray cardigan, pulling it on over my tank top and red underwear. There are four of them, but the prophecy says *five*.

At the top of the stairs, I look down into the living room, expecting to see Luther asleep on the couch. He's not there. I pad quietly down, then cross the room to the kitchen. His empty whiskey glass is still in the sink, and now the whiskey bottle is empty too. How much did he freaking drink last night?

After drinking down a glass of water, I fill the kettle and put it on the stove.

I'm spooning coffee into a mug when the door opens, and Luther enters. He's covered in sweat, wearing running shorts and a gray vest that clings to his torso. His arms bulge as he leans onto his knees to catch his breath. When he notices me, he stands up straight and reaches for a towel that's hanging on a hook by the door.

"Running off the hangover?" I glance at the whiskey bottle.

Luther doesn't reply, just pushes past me, grabs a glass, and fills it with tap water. As he drinks it down, I watch his throat. The movement of his Adam's apple sends a fizzing sensation through my veins. I look away and turn back to the kettle.

After a moment's silence, I say, "Have you and Mack made up yet?"

"We're fine," he replies gruffly.

Turning around, I lean on the counter and fold my arms in front of my stomach. Luther's eyes flit to my chest, then my legs, catching on my red underwear. I pull my cardigan closed around my middle, and he looks away. "You don't seem fine." I raise my eyebrows at him then shake my head. "I don't get it, Luther. What's going on? Why are you so against me going to the gala? You took me to *Spine*; you didn't mind that."

"*Spine* wasn't crawling with Bureau agents who want your blood."

"And you care because...?"

He frowns.

"Luther, you don't even like me, so why do you give a crap?" I step forward, glaring up at him.

"Because you're supposed to save the world, and I think Mack is being pretty careless with you, that's why."

"Right." I roll my eyes. "Careless with me? Like I'm a delicate vase he might break?"

"Not delicate. Precious. There's a difference." Luther's gaze catches mine. Heat quivers between us. For a second, just one quick second, I see the guy who shared his secrets with me in the dark, but then he's gone. As the kettle boils, he storms out of the kitchen and heads straight for the bathroom. When he slams the door behind him, it makes the pictures rattle on the walls.

8

LUTHER

I don't even need to turn the water to hot. As soon as I pull the handle on the shower, the fire inside me heats it to boiling point. Steam fills the room. I brace my hands on the sink and mutter, "Fuck."

Molten arousal rushes through my veins. The way she looked at me. The way she stood there, red panties peeking out from the hem of her black top. Bare legs. Crumpled, just-woke-up skin.

I pull my hand back and punch the mirror. Hard. It shatters. Pieces fall into the sink.

I'm furious with Mack for thinking putting her at risk is a good idea, and I'm furious with her for the things she does to me. The way she makes me feel. I want her so much I can hardly breathe when she's near me. Like there's no air left in the room if she's in it.

As my cock stiffens in my shorts, I pull open the cupboard below the sink. At the back, behind Tanner's array of hair products, is a small black wash bag. I take it out and unzip it. Thrusting my hand inside, I groan as my fingers meet smooth fabric. Disgusted with myself, but so fucking turned on I can't stop, I take Nova's underwear out of the bag. The underwear she gave me when I went shopping for our outfits. The underwear I never gave back.

Tugging down my shorts, I give my cock a long, firm stroke. I picture her kneeling in front of me, opening her mouth. As my hand picks up speed, I press her panties to my face and inhale.

"What the fuck?" Her voice makes me stop—caught in a hilariously awful freeze frame. My back is facing her, but she can see me in the pieces of shattered mirror that still cling to the wall. "Luther? What the fuck?"

She steps inside and pushes the door closed behind her. Before it seals shut, a cloud of steam escapes, clearing the air between us.

With her underwear still clasped in my hand, I pull my shorts up and turn to face her.

Humiliation burns on my skin. I can't interpret the look on her face. If she's horrified that she just caught me jerking off while sniffing her stolen panties, she isn't showing it.

Our eyes meet. She lets go of her cardigan and allows it to hang open. Her chest is moving quickly up and down, her breath short and heavy. I let her underwear fall from my hand then, before I can stop myself, I lunge for her. I hold her face, pull her lips to mine. They're hot and urgent. I slam her back against the wall. She grabs my vest and tugs it over my head, then runs her hands over my abs. When she reaches my nipples, she dips her head and makes hot, wet circles with her tongue.

I weave my fingers into her hair, a shuddering sigh leaving my mouth. Then I jerk her head back and steal her lips with mine. Steam fills the room again. I can barely see her.

Her skin is so warm, so fucking warm, and now I'm desperate to know how warm the rest of her is.

I pull her cardigan off her arms then haul her top over her head. As her breasts bounce free, my cock strains against my shorts. I'm so hard it's almost painful. My balls are throbbing. Not just my balls… the spot deep inside me, behind them, is pulsing.

I move my hands to her red panties. I'm about to peel them off her when she says, "No. Just fuck me."

Fire dances in her eyes. Sparks merge with steam, and I have no idea if they're hers or mine or a mixture of both.

I don't need to be told twice. As she frees my cock, I lift her into my arms. "I'm too heavy," she whispers, vulnerability flashing in her eyes.

"Shut the fuck up," I tell her. "Just wrap your legs around me."

As she hooks her knees around my waist, my fingers find her pussy. I massage her clit then, while she moans into my mouth, I slam up into her. She gasps, her eyes widening at the feel of the metal on my shaft.

"It's pierced?" she says. "I've never—"

The thought that I'm giving her something no one else ever has makes me wild with lust. I roar a guttural roar and push her back harder against the wall.

Digging her nails into my shoulders, she stays still while I thrust up into her, my ladder of metal stroking her inside walls.

She's so wet and so hot, and she takes me so well that I feel like I'm going to come within seconds. Dropping her to the floor, so she's standing, I spin her around and pull her panties off. She juts out her ass. For a second, as I run my hands over her cheeks, I wonder what it would feel like to push my pierced shaft past her tight ring of muscle. But she's not ready for that.

Instead, I thrust back into her cunt. She pushes onto me, bracing her hands on the wall. With one hand, I reach for her clit. With the other, I pinch her nipple until she squeals. I wring an orgasm from her, but she doesn't pull away from me.

"Again." She grabs my hand, keeps it on her pussy. "Make me come again."

So, I keep touching her. This time, I change the angle of my hips until she cries out and jerks forward. "Is that it?" I growl. "Is that the spot?"

Nova doesn't reply. She's quivering, as if she's scared to move in case the sensation disappears.

This time, we come together. When liquid heat fills me up and electric shocks devour my body, she trembles on my cock, and leans back into my chest while reaching up to hook her arm around my neck. I hold her close. Her body is fire, burning my skin, sending pleasure and pain ricocheting through my muscles.

I stroke her damp hair from her neck. I want to lower my lips to her shoulder and kiss her hot skin, but she pulls away before I get the chance.

When my cock leaves her, everything feels cold. Too cold. I stagger back, thinking about the hot cum that must be leaking out of her as she stands up straight.

Without saying anything, Nova slowly turns around and picks up the underwear I stole from her. Her face is flushed. Her pupils wide and dark. She's so delicious I want to pull her into the shower with me and watch the water cascade over her hips as I help wash my cum from her pussy.

Silently, she puts on the panties she caught me burying my face in. She clasps her bra around her torso and pulls it up to cover her breasts. Then she leaves.

As clouds of steam leave with her, and the room clears, I realize she's left something behind; she's left her red underwear on the floor.

I'm just not sure if she left it by accident.

9

SAM

Nova emerges from the bathroom wearing nothing but black panties and a bra. The shower is running, but neither her hair nor body is wet. When she meets my eyes, a playful grin crosses her face. She's glowing. Literally glowing.

"Fire Daddy?" I ask conspiratorially.

Nova nods, pulling her black tank top and cardigan back on. "He's... pierced." She wiggles her eyebrows. Her cheeks are pink.

I glance toward the bathroom door. "I thought he hated you?" I follow her to the kitchen where she puts the kettle on the stove. There's already one mug on the counter. She takes another from the cupboard.

"Maybe he was trying to fuck the human out of me," she quips.

I glance toward the bathroom. The shower has stopped. "Told you he's number five," I mutter as Luther emerges.

Avoiding looking at us, he clears his throat and perches on a stool the other side of the counter. "Can I...?" he asks, gesturing to the coffee.

Nova nods. "Of course." She sets out a third mug. "You like it sweet?"

"However it comes," he replies, meeting her eyes. "As long as it's hot and wet."

As the air grows warmer, I wait in anticipation, caught between laughing and feeling totally turned on. I'm kind of hoping that they'll go for round two, and allow me to watch, but then the others appear the top of the stairs and the moment is broken.

One after the other, Kole, Tanner, and Mack join us in the kitchen. Nova makes everyone coffee. Tanner's face tells me he feels something different between Nova and Luther but instead of asking what it is, he just settles onto a stool next to Luther and watches the two of them as he sips his coffee.

"So, are we decided?" Mack looks around the group. "Nova and I will go to the gala?"

There's silence for a moment. Luther's jaw twitches.

"I don't like it," says Kole. "But after what we saw..." He glances at Nova. "I think Mack's right. We either need the Bureau to back off or we need them to help us. Annalise is our best shot at that."

Nova nods in agreement. "I think so too."

Pushing his floppy hair from his face, Tanner sighs. To Mack he says, "I wish there was another way but, right now, I can't think of one. So, yeah, I think you should go."

"Sam?" Mack turns to me.

I get a vote? I've been here less than five minutes; the idea that they care what I think is surprising but welcome. "I trust Nova." I squeeze her elbow. "If she thinks this is the right thing to do, then I trust her."

Finally looking at Luther, Mack extends his hand. "It's settled," he says.

Luther examines Mack's outstretched palm. For a moment, I think he's going to storm off again, but he doesn't.

This time, he relents. Shaking Mack's hand, he pulls him in for a brotherly hug and claps him on the back. When they're done, Luther stalks over to the living room. We all join him with our coffees and sit down while Mack paces in front of us like the professor he is.

"The gala is tonight. Seven thirty. Solleville." He stops and puts his hands into his pockets, then glances at Nova. "We can mask our appearance. It's a hard spell, and it won't last long, but it should last long enough to get us in front of Annalise."

"It works the same way as masking the cabin?" Nova asks.

Cutting in, Tanner says, "Pretty much. You're not invisible, you're just making people see something different."

"They can't detect that stuff?" I ask, wrapping my hands around my mug.

Mack tilts his head to the side. "They'll have security on the doors, but that's why we need a distraction." Hesitantly, he adds, "We need Sarah's help."

"Sarah?" My stomach tightens. "Why?"

Mack sits down on the coffee table opposite me, leaning onto his knees. "Sarah's a complete unknown. The Bureau has no idea she's connected to us. Plus, we're pretty sure we can trust her." He pauses and looks at Luther, who nods in agreement.

"What would you need her to do?" I ask, my mouth dry.

"Sarah's an unelemental witch." Mack cocks his head. "Did you know that?"

I frown. No, I didn't know that.

"It means she has no affinity. She can't cast spells or incantations without a wand, but wands aren't permitted at events like this." Mack sits up. "All we'd need her to do is try to get past security and make a bit of a fuss about the unfair treatment of unelementals when they tell her she has to leave the wand at the door. Give us chance to slip past them."

"That's the plan?" Luther says darkly. "Slip past them?"

"Yes," Mack replies. "That's the plan."

As Luther rolls his eyes, Kole says, "It could work." He rubs his long dark beard. "This isn't a high-security event. It's a fundraiser. If Sarah creates enough of a distraction, Mack and Nova can take the chance to get in without the masking spells being detected. Then all they need to do is find Annalise."

"Which is easy," Mack says, reaching into his pocket for his phone, "because she's giving the keynote speech at eight p.m." He turns his phone so we can see the screen. A picture of a tall, dark-haired woman with bright red lips fills the screen. "I'll let my mask down for a few seconds, so she can spot me in the audience. That'll be enough." Mack puts the phone away. "If she sees me, sees what I've risked to be there, she'll meet with us." He turns to Nova. "She'll help us."

Nova drums her fingernails on her coffee cup. "Okay," she says, "then you better teach me how to do this masking spell."

10

MACK

When Rev answers the phone, it's obvious she was sleeping. I hear rustling noises that tell me she's sitting up in bed. "By the moon, Mack. It's nine a.m. Tanner and Kole have only been gone a few hours."

"I know. I'm sorry."

"What's going on?" she asks, a little more awake now.

While Rev listens intently, I explain what we're planning to do. If she thinks it's a bad idea, she doesn't say so. "I'm sorry to involve you again," I tell her. "I didn't want you to have to come back out here. That's why Tanner and Kole came to you."

"It's okay, Mack. I want to help." She's walking around now. I hear closets and drawers opening. "What time do you need to leave for the city?"

"Six."

"Then I'll be with you at five, just after sunset. I'll bring outfits for you both, and I'll bring Sarah."

"You're sure she'll be okay with it?"

"The woman's riddled with guilt for lying to Nova. She'd do anything to make it up to her." Rev pauses. "Plus, she's desperate to see Sam. You'll give them a minute together? Before we leave?"

"Of course." I pinch the bridge of my nose. "Of course, I will."

"Good. Then I'll see you at five." And with that, she hangs up.

I'm staring down into the deep blue water of the lake when I sense Nova walking toward me. Snow would know her scent at a hundred paces, but as she draws closer the air changes. Grows warmer. Starts to vibrate. Most of the time, my elemental affinity is drowned out by the shifter part of me. But lately, when Nova's around, it's grown stronger.

"Everything okay?" she asks, sitting down next to me.

She's changed into jeans and a large black hoodie that belongs to Kole. It drowns her, but she looks tantalizingly cute inside it. "Rev's on board. She'll be here at five with Sarah and our outfits."

Nova smiles a little. "At least this outfit won't be as risqué as the last one I had to wear."

Thinking of her in the ensemble Luther picked out— because Tanner showed me the photo and, of course, I couldn't *not* look—my cock twitches. I clear my throat. "Definitely less revealing," I tell her.

"You trust Rev, don't you?" she asks, swinging her legs gently over the side of the jetty.

"I've known her a long time." As Nova shivers, I edge closer and put my arm around her. Snow grumbles protectively in my head. He was *not* happy when Luther accused me of putting Nova in danger. We would give our life for her; Luther should know that.

Nova reaches for my hand and entwines her fingers with mine. "Tell me something," she says softly.

"What kind of something?"

"Something about you." She looks up at me.

I laugh nervously and rub my beard with my free hand. "Okay... I'm a shifter. A polar bear lives inside my body and my head. I'm an air mage. I worked for the Bureau as an agent and then a teacher. I was the town's sheriff before they suspended me... you know all this, Nova."

Tilting her head, shrugging out of my grasp, she says, "Tell me something about *you*, Mack. Not your work or something everyone else knows." Moving her hand to her chest, where Kole's ink hides that hideous fucking mark her now-dead-boyfriend left on her, she blinks at me. Her eyes are wide. The contrast between blue and brown is hypnotizing. "You know me, Mack. Not all of my past, but a lot of it." She sits back on the jetty and crosses her legs. "I know more about *Luther* than I know about you."

A frown creases my forehead. Luther? Luther's been sharing deep, dark secrets with her?

Noticing the look on my face, Nova's lips twitch into a smile. "I tell you what... if you share something with me—something *real*—I'll share a secret with you." She taps her foot. "It's a good one, you'll be pleased to know it."

Studying her face, a mixture of trepidation and happiness blooms in my chest. How does she do this? How does she manage to make everything seem better? Lighter? "All right." I turn away from her and look out at the lake. There's one truth I want to share with her, but it's the kind of conversation that tends to dampen the mood.

A solemn weight settles on my shoulders as I say, "It's not true that you know nothing about me."

Nova doesn't speak. The air is still.

"You know that my sister died." I focus on the horizon. "Her name was Layla. She was just a little younger than you. I was her big brother." My mouth is dry. I swallow forcefully. Turning back to look at Nova, I force out the words I rarely say to anyone. "Layla took her own life."

I watch as Nova's eyes widen. A look of utter sorrow passes over her face. "Mack—"

"Rev was Layla's best friend. She found her at The Hollow." I stop. Nova doesn't need to know any more than that.

Nova takes my hand in hers, then reaches up and strokes the side of my face. I lean into her warmth. A breeze blows across the surface of the lake. I'm losing control of my emotions. It whips up through the trees. Above us, storm clouds gather. Snow is pacing in my head. He misses Layla the same way I do. He lets out a sad growl as I screw my eyes shut and try to lock the grief back inside.

"I'm sorry." Nova kisses my neck. "I'm truly sorry."

For a long moment, we sit beside one another, not speaking or moving. I listen to her breath moving in and out of her chest. The rhythm soothes the pounding in my temples. Finally, when I'm able to speak, I squeeze her hand and say, "Your turn." I smile, trying to lighten the heavy mood that has settled on us. "You promised to share something. Something I'll be *pleased* to know."

Sitting back, Nova shakes her head. "It's childish. I shouldn't have pushed you."

"Nova…" I catch her chin with my index finger and make her look at me. "I'm glad I told you." I sit back and fold my arms. "But now it's your turn. You promised me a secret, Little Star."

Hearing her nickname on my lips, Nova smiles. "All right." Something dances across her face. With bright eyes, she drums her fingers on her thighs. "Guess who I caught this morning, jerking off in the bathroom?"

I frown, thinking back to our movements when we woke up. Nova disappeared first then Sam. But seeing Sam wouldn't be something worth sharing. I raise my eyebrows. "Luther?"

Nova nods eagerly. "Mm hmm, and guess what he was burying his face in while he did it?"

I have no idea what she's about to say.

"My underwear." She folds her arms a little indignantly. "My underwear! He took them with him when he went to buy our *Spine* outfits and never gave them back."

My mouth hangs open a little. A chuckle ripples my chest. It starts small then grows until I'm laughing so hard my eyes water. "Fuck," I breathe. "I don't know why that's so funny."

"It's not funny!" Nova nudges me in the ribs.

"Of course, it is. He's in love with you. He just too fucking pig-headed to admit it." I wipe my eyes and shake my head. "Which explains why he was so mad at me for suggesting you come with me to speak to Annalise."

"In love with me?" Nova tuts. "No. He's not. Sure, he'll throw me up against a wall but—"

"Against a wall?" Something tugs at my chest. Jealousy? No. It can't be. I don't feel jealous when I watch her with the others. I feel safe. Home. Like that's how it's supposed to be.

Nova nods.

Looking at her, wide eyed and small in Kole's giant hoodie, I have the urge to pull her close and never let go. I want to kiss her. I want to lie her down, out here in the open, and kiss every inch of her.

Instead, I stand up and offer her my hand. When she stands too, she narrows her eyes at me. "Are you mad?"

"No."

"But you're something? Jealous?" She hops in front of me. "Are you jealous, Daddy?"

"No, I'm not jealous." Fuck, I can hardly resist her when she calls me that.

After a pause, as we start walking, she says, "You think Luther's in love with me?"

"Yes, I do."

"And you think he's being pig-headed for not admitting it?"

"Stubborn is Luther's middle name," I say, shoving my hands into my pockets.

"What about you?" Nova stops walking. I turn back to look at her. Her hands are on her hips.

"Me?"

"You haven't told me how *you* feel about me." She steps closer, closing the gap between us. In a husky tone, she says, "You won't even let yourself fuck me."

"Nova—"

"Why are you still holding back?" She puts her hand on my hip, then slowly moves it to the front of my pants. As she applies pressure, I swell into her hand. "Why won't you give in when you want it so badly?"

I catch her hand with mine. "It's just a line I can't cross, Nova." I step away from her. "I'm sorry." I start walking back toward the cabin. "I just can't."

"You'll do all that other stuff, but you won't fuck me?" Nova darts in front of me. "Mack, that's ridiculous."

"It's for your own good," I tell her.

For a moment, I think she's going to challenge me further but the fire fades from her eyes. The dejection that replaces it as she slips her hand into mine is worse. It almost breaks my heart. Snow growls at me. *You know I'm right*, I tell him silently. *You know I'll only hurt her.*

Snow doesn't reply.

11

NOVA

While we wait for Rev to arrive with our things, I find Tanner and Sam. The three of us play cards and they're doing a good job of trying to stay cheerful, but they can tell something's wrong. After my bathroom moment with Luther, and what happened on the jetty with Mack, my brain is fizzing. Except, not in a good way.

Having sex with Luther was incredibly hot. Both literally and figuratively. But I have no idea where it leaves us or what it meant.

Hearing Mack open up to me a little was what I thought I needed from him, but when he said he'd never cross *that* line with me—never actually allow himself to be inside me—I was filled with such sadness I could barely breathe.

Tanner told me once that Mack deserves happiness. The problem is, I don't think Mack feels the same. He carries the guilt of his sister's death like a heavy weight around his neck, and I don't know how to convince him that she wouldn't want him to be so sad. So alone.

I know I wouldn't. If it was Sam, I wouldn't want him to be alone.

Glancing at Sam as he and Tanner exchange a flirtatious glance that makes my skin tingle, I examine his face. We're not family. Not really. The way I feel about him certainly isn't the way you'd feel about your *actual* brother. But he's still the closest link I've got to my past.

Catching me looking at him, he leans over for a kiss. I let him wrap his arm around my waist, growing hungrier as he pulls me to him.

"Hey, come on." Tanner raps his knuckles on the table. "Let's at least finish this hand before we..." He waves at us. "Get handsy."

Laughing, wiping my wet lips coyly with the back of my hand, I slip back into my chair. We continue playing for a while, but before I know what time it is, Kole's in the living room telling us that Mack and Luther have gone to meet Rev and bring her to the cabin.

Instantly, Sam's face pales. He puts his cards down and looks at Tanner, who nods at him. "It'll be okay, buddy," Tanner says. "It's going to be fine. When you see her, it'll all be fine."

"Tanner's right." I squeeze Sam's leg under the table. "This is a happy moment, Sam." I fix my eyes on his. "It's a good thing."

After a few minutes, with Sam nervously pacing up and down while I sit with Tanner and Kole and try to think of things to say that will calm his nerves, we hear voices outside. Sam sits down on the couch, then stands, then sits again. When the door opens, he jolts to his feet and strides toward it. He stops in the middle of the room.

Mack enters first, then Luther, with Rev coming in behind them. When she spots me, she comes straight over for a hug. She smells wonderful, but instead of her customary bright clothing she's dressed all in black. We stand to the side as Sarah enters.

She looks the same. Exactly the same. Long silver hair, pale eyes, and smooth skin with delicate wrinkles. I try to meet her eyes, but it's like all she can see is Sam. She moves slowly toward him as if she's floating. She's already crying. Big, thick tears roll down her cheeks. She stops in front of him, reaches out her arms, then takes them back and hugs herself with them. "Oh," she mutters. "My beautiful boy. How grown up you look."

A million emotions cross Sam's face. I glance at Tanner. He's rubbing his temples. "Sorry," he says. "I need some air." He ducks out of the room and Kole follows him.

"Sarah?" Sam whispers her name then suddenly lurches forward and wraps his arms around her. Lifting her up, he spins her around. She starts laughing and thumps his shoulders.

When he puts her down, she cups his face in her hands. "I never forgot you," she says. "All this time, I was looking for you."

"I know." Sam squeezes her hands between his. "I know you were."

Finally, Sarah remembers I'm here. Holding onto Sam, like she's afraid he'll disappear, she turns to me. "Nova, I'm so sorry." Reluctantly, she pulls out of Sam's grasp and crosses the room. "I'm so very sorry. Everything I did—"

"Everything you did was for Sam." I reach out and pat her arm. "It's okay. I understand."

As Sarah starts to cry again and returns to Sam, Rev tips her head in the direction of the stairs. "Somewhere we can get you ready?" she asks. She's holding two bags.

"Sure," I tell her.

Handing one of the bags to Mack, Rev says, "This is for you. Don't ask how I got a tux at such short notice. Long story." Holding up the other bag, she says to me, "This one's yours. Let's go get you dolled up, shall we?"

* * *

IN THE BEDROOM, I sit on a stool in front of the dressing table and let Rev apply more makeup than I've ever worn in my life.

"Why do I need this if I'm using a masking spell? Can't I just make people think I'm wearing makeup and fancy clothes?"

"It doesn't work like that," Rev chuckles. "It hides your true face, makes people see someone else, but it can't make them see what's not there."

"That makes no sense," I laugh.

"Magick rarely does." Rev stands back to appraise the mascara she just applied to my lashes. "Hair now," she says, taking a pair of curling tongs from the bag.

In the corner of the room, the dress she brought me is hanging long and loose. It's a stunningly beautiful emerald green with a neckline I know will flatter my cleavage.

When Rev has finished with my hair, she combs her fingers through the curls to loosen them. Then she sprays me with a cloud of hairspray. "Time to put your dress on," she says, stepping back proudly.

She turns away as I remove my clothes and step into the dress. When I've pulled it up, I ask her to help with the zip. She slides it up, adjusts the straps for me, then turns me around. "Fuck," she says, grinning. "You look good, Nova. Really good."

"I'd say maybe Mack won't be able to resist me, but I know he will." I peer into the mirror, wondering how Rev has managed to make my eyes look so large.

"Resist you?" Rev sits on the foot of the bed. "I thought you two…? I thought all four of you…?"

"With Mack, it seems like it's complicated." I sit back down on the stool. "He'll only go so far. He says he can't cross the line." I shake my head and sigh.

Rev studies me for a moment then stands up. Gesturing for me to follow her, she heads for the stairs. "Listen," she says, "Rhone Mackenzie is one of the best men I know, but he's spent over twenty years blaming himself for what happened to Layla."

"He told me," I say quietly.

"It wasn't his fault." Rev's lips settle in a tight line. "The Hollow has always been a bad place. Bad energy. I've always believed it drove Layla to…" She hesitates. "To do what she did." We're at the top of the stairs when Rev squeezes my hand. "Just give him time," she says. Then she winks at me. "Failing that, give him orders."

I frown at her. Heat colors my cheeks as the memory of Mack tied to his armchair burns in my brain. "How did you know…?"

Rev taps her forehead. "I'm a seer. I see things. It's in the job description." Then she trots down the stairs ahead of me, leaving me to make my big entrance.

1 2

MACK

As I straighten my bowtie, Tanner pats my arm.

"You look good, brother," Kole says, nodding in agreement.

"Bit more dignified than Luther when he took our girl out, that's for sure," Tanner adds, stealing an amused glance at Luther. He's holding a whiskey glass again. Clearly, fucking Nova up against the bathroom wall hasn't gotten her out of his system.

Turning back to Tanner, I say, "As long as we pass for guests."

"Here's your ticket." Sam is at the kitchen counter, holding my phone. "I downloaded it for you. Nova's too."

I peer at the screen.

"Sarah, Rev has yours I think." Sam gestures to the stairs where Rev has appeared. She trots down the steps into the living room, smiling. When she reaches me, she folds her arms and nods approvingly. "Looking fine, professor," she says. "But not as fine as your girl."

Hearing Rev call Nova my girl sends a gentle vibration

63

through me. Snow is purring. Internally, I roll my eyes at him.

When I look up, though, my breath catches in my chest. Nova is practically gliding down the stairs. Her figure wrapped in emerald-green silk that seems to hug and accentuate every curve of her delicious body, she is radiant.

Tanner whistles, Sam mutters, "Holy hell," and Kole simply growls from somewhere deep in his chest. When I look at him, he's licking his lower lip. For once, I'd have to agree that she looks good enough to eat.

"Well?" Nova smooths the fabric over her hips. She looks nervous and it makes me wish that—just for one second— she could see herself the way we see her. "Will I do?"

From the corner of the room, Luther is watching her. I ignore him, take her hand, and kiss it the way I did when we very first met. "You'll do very nicely," I tell her.

Smiling at me, she drops my hand and moves into the center of a Sam, Tanner, Kole circle. Tanner brushes her hair from her neck and whispers to her that he likes it curled. Sam's hand lingers on her ass. Kole can't stop staring at his ink work, proudly displayed on her chest. Catching him looking at it, she strokes his beard and says, "When I get back, there's another tattoo you need to cover for me." She glances down at her thigh. Kole nods, his lips in a tight line; we all know which tattoo she's talking about and I know for a fact that every time one of us sees it, we want to scrub it clean from her skin.

"Consider it done," Kole says in his gravelly tone.

Finally, Luther stands and walks over to us. "You know the spell?" he asks her, folding his arms.

"I know the spell," Nova replies tightly.

"You're travelling separately?" Luther glances from me to Rev.

"We are," Rev replies. Turning to me, she asks, "Ready?"

"Ready." I rest my hand on the small of Nova's back. As we head outside, she says goodbye to the others. They hug her, kiss her, and whisper things to her as if they're truly worried it might be the last time they see her. "I'll keep her safe," I tell them.

"We know you will, brother," Kole says, patting my upper arm. "See you soon."

At the bottom of the steps, Nova, Rev, and I wait for Sam to say his own goodbye to Sarah. He stays strong, but Sarah is wiping tears from her face when she turns away from him.

"Thank you for helping us," I say to her as we move through the trees toward the turnout where our vehicles are parked—just inside the mask.

"It's the least I could do," Sarah sniffs.

"You won't be in danger," I promise her. "Rev will be looking out for you."

"I know." Sarah nods. "I'm happy to do it."

When we reach the turnout, Rev and Sarah climb into Rev's beaten-up old Honda and pull away first so they can be in position when Nova and I get there.

We're taking the truck. The one the guys stole on their escape from The Hollow. Still masked, thankfully.

I offer Nova my hand as she climbs up into the passenger seat. By the moon, I wish I was taking her out properly tonight. Going to some fancy event with her on my arm because I'm trying to woo her not because I'm trying to prevent her being put in jail by the Bureau.

When I start up the engine, she inhales deeply as if she's stealing herself for what's to come.

"It's going to be okay," I tell her. "Worst comes to worst, Snow will get us the fuck out of there."

She turns and smiles at me. "I know he will."

"Nova, about earlier—"

"It's okay, Mack. We can talk about it later." She

straightens up in her seat, hands in her lap. After a beat of silence, she looks at me sideways and adds, "You look good, by the way." A smile flutters on her lips. "Really good."

Seeing her look at me that way sends a shiver of arousal down my spine. It shouldn't. Especially now, I shouldn't be thinking about all the things I want to do to her in that dress. I shouldn't be thinking about how much I want to see her beautiful face become flushed and sweaty while I'm buried between her thighs. I shouldn't be wishing she'd ignore what I told her about only going so far. Tie me up again. *Make* me give in to her.

Adjusting my pants, I try to focus on what we're about to do. I've run through the steps at least one hundred times. Sarah causes a distraction, we slip past the spell detectors, then make it to the front of the audience where I drop my mask long enough for Annalise to notice me. After that, it's all unknowns. What I'm hoping is that Annalise will sense the urgency in my face and find a way for us to meet. As a backup plan, however, Snow is ready to let all hell loose on the gala and break us out if he has to.

"Is Sam doing okay?" I glance at Nova. I can't sit here in silence for the next forty minutes. We have to talk about *something* or my mind will wander and I'll start thinking about all the wrong things.

"He's been through a lot," Nova replies, biting her lower lip. "He wants to put it behind him, but there's a lot he needs to process." She rubs her forearms as if she's suddenly feeling chilled. "I get that. I mean, I didn't really have time to process before I met you guys but—"

"Any time you need to talk to me." I'm speaking urgently. The thought of her still suffering—feeling in any way hurt or damaged by what that monster Johnny put her through— makes me sick to my stomach. "Any time... I'm here, Nova."

"Same," she says quickly, fixing her eyes on me with a heat

that makes me feel like I'm standing in direct sunlight. "I'm here, Mack. If *you* need to talk."

After that, I flick on the radio. I find a station that's playing music and crank it up. Nova taps her fingers on her thigh in time to the music.

Half an hour later, we reach Solleville. I know the hotel because when I was an agent, and then a teacher at the Academy, I attended the gala every year. Usually, I was forced to make a speech or schmooze wealthy donors. Rev's car is already in the parking lot. There are two entrances. The one up top is for people who want to be photographed. The one down below, opposite where we've parked, is more subtle. It's tempting to go for the latter, but we need the attention of the press.

Nova and I wait for Sarah to get out of the car. Rev stays put, ready to drive away as soon as Sarah's finished her dramatic performance.

As Sarah heads for the stairwell that leads up to the main entrance at the front of the hotel, Nova and I follow a few paces behind. Up top, we wait in the shadows. When Sarah approaches the doors with Rev's cell phone in her hand, displaying her ticket, we perform our masking spells.

The ease with which Nova is picking up these new spells is both impressive and disarming. She's never been around magick, never even knew how to tap into her elemental affinity until a few weeks ago. Yet, she's almost quicker than me already. She shakes her hair and flexes her jaw. "My skin feels tingly and tight," she says. "Is it supposed to feel that way?"

I tilt my head from side to side. "Sounds about right," I tell her.

"What do I look like?" she asks, looking up at me.

I study her face. I've always found masking people a strange experience. In many ways, Nova's the same. Green dress, curly silver hair. But her face is different. Her features aren't her own. Her eyes are now dark brown, and her lips aren't right either. If I saw her in a crowd, my eyes would catch on her and I'd think, *Oh, that's Nova.* But the second she turned to me I'd realize I'd made a mistake.

"Different," I tell her. "Not you."

"Same." She reaches up and strokes the side of my face. "I don't like it," she says. "Where has my Mack gone?"

My heart thuds faster in my chest. *Hers.* I'm hers?

Ahead of us, at the entrance, Sarah reaches the checkpoint. She opens her arms and stands with her feet apart to be body scanned. Immediately, the alarms go off. She's asked to empty her purse. When she takes out her wand, the security guard gruffly explains they're not permitted inside. I hold my breath, praying she can muster the required level of outrage.

As it turns out, she's a better actress than I imagined she'd be. In a loud, wailing voice, she begins to shout. When she gets to the part about unelementals still being treated like second class citizens, the reporters with cameras start to take notice. A crowd forms. Another unelemental steps forward and starts yelling, too. Sarah turns and starts speaking directly to the journalists. They frantically take pictures. A flurry of security guards appears.

I grab Nova's arm. "This is it," I tell her. "Show time."

While almost every security guard on duty tries to calm the crazed unelemental out front, we join the queue. Absent-mindedly, someone scans our tickets, but the spell scanner is obscured by Sarah and her display.

"Shall we wait?" I ask, tipping my head toward the scanner.

"No. Just go," the guard says hurriedly, ushering us inside. "Less people out here the better."

I hold my breath until we're through the foyer and standing in the main hall.

"We did it," Nova breathes. "We're in."

"We're in." I squeeze her waist, then she loops her arm through mine.

On stage, a band is playing gentle jazz music. People are dancing, sipping champagne from tall glasses, and nibbling on ridiculously tiny appetizers as they wait for the keynote speech to start.

"What do we do now?" Nova asks.

"Now?" I extend my hand and bow a little. "We dance."

* * *

WORKING our way through the crowd, I lead Nova to a spot near the stage.

"I don't know how to..." She trails off, looking nervously at the couples around us who are dancing waltz-style in one another's arms.

Taking her right hand with my left, I put my other hand on her waist and pull her closer. Instinctively, she rests her left hand on my upper arm. "That's it," I tell her. "Don't worry about your feet, just move to the music."

Instead of looking up at me, as if she doesn't want to stare into the eyes of someone who doesn't look like the real me, Nova rests her head on my chest. I sigh as her heart beats against mine. She is warm, and soft, and smooth in my arms. Moving slowly, so I can keep one eye on the large clock above the stage, I breathe in her scent. In another time and place, this would be like heaven.

"You look beautiful," I tell her. "You're always beautiful but tonight—in that dress—you are..." I trail off. Nova has nudged her hips forward, and the contact has taken my breath away. "Nova," I growl, glancing at the clock, "it's nearly time."

I've barely finished speaking when the band stops playing. The crowd quiets. The lights change to brighten around the room. A voiceover says, "Distinguished guests, we won't keep you long, we know you want to return to the music and the drinks…" A ripple of laughter moves through the crowd. "But first, it is our great pleasure to introduce to the stage The Supernatural Defense Bureau's Associate Deputy Director, Annalise Kellerman!"

13

NOVA

Applause breaks out as Mack inches me closer to the stage. He doesn't *look* like Mack, but he feels like Mack, and he smells like Mack. And the feel of him in his tux, dancing with me, was so intoxicating I almost forgot why we're here.

There's a click of heels, a swish of a curtain, and then Annalise Kellerman appears from backstage. Watching her sashay toward the microphone, my stomach drops. She's stunning—dark brown hair, bright red lips, ice-blue eyes. She's wearing a black dress that clings to her near-perfect figure. When she reaches the front of the stage, she stops and waits for the applause to die down.

Mack takes my hand in his and squeezes it.

Annalise starts talking, commanding the room with ease and confidence. She thanks the audience, the donors, and names several outreach programs and community projects. When it seems she's drawing near the end of her speech, Mack lets go of me.

I glance at him. A shudder runs through his body. Then he's Mack again. His features, his eyes, his hair, his beard. He stares at the stage. My heartbeat quickens. What if she doesn't see him? What if someone else sees him and recognizes him?

A tense moment passes then, as if something in the air has shifted and she's trying to figure out what it is, Annalise's gaze sweeps across the crowd.

When her eyes reach Mack, she stumbles over her words. She blinks several times before correcting herself and looking away from him.

As she finishes her speech, her eyes dart constantly to Mack's face. The crowd is applauding her, and she's about to walk off stage, when she catches his eyes and gives the smallest nod of her head.

Instantly, Mack replaces his mask and grabs my hand. He pulls me across the dancefloor, weaving through the audience, following Annalise. We reach the steps at the side of the stage at the exact moment she does. She glides down them, shaking hands with others who are waiting to introduce themselves to her. Mack waits in line, positioning me just behind him. When Annalise reaches him, she shakes his hand like she shook everyone else's. But then she leans in. Her lips move close to his ear. As she straightens herself, Mack nods. Then she's gone, disappearing through a door at the back of the room.

"What did she say?" I ask as Mack leads me toward the drinks table.

Grabbing us each a glass of champagne, he stands still and scans the room. "Third floor, ten minutes."

"What's on the third floor?" I ask.

"Presidential suite," Mack replies.

Before I have the chance to ask how he knows where the presidential suite is, he's downed his champagne and is gesturing to the foyer. "We can't go straight there. Best if it looks like we're checking into a room." He holds out his arm and I take it.

In the foyer, we head for the reception desk. Mack leans forward and conspiratorially says, "My secretary and I would like a room please. Just for a few hours."

"I really shouldn't—" The concierge begins to answer, but Mack pushes his hand across the desk. When he lifts it, he reveals a wad of hundred-dollar bills. I can't even count how many are there.

"If we can keep it off the books?" Mack raises his eyebrows.

Smirking, the concierge pockets the cash and takes a keycard from beneath the counter. "Of course, Sir."

"I'll return this before the end of the night," Mack promises him.

"Room 408," the man says, giving me a lecherous look that makes my skin crawl.

Nodding, Mack hooks his arm around my waist and makes a show of hustling me into the elevator. Inside, he turns to me and says, "Are you okay?"

"I'm fine." I squeeze his hand. "Don't worry."

He stares at me for a moment, like he's trying to look past the spell and see my real face. "I miss your eyes," he says, touching his thumb to the side of my face.

I run my hands up his arms. "I miss yours too." I'm about to stretch up and kiss him when we arrive on the fourth floor. "I thought you said Annalise is on the third floor?"

Mack nods, exiting the elevator. "She is, but the concierge needs to think we went to the fourth." He waggles the keycard at me. "And that we entered our room. He's greedy but not stupid. He'll be checking his system."

Inside the hotel room, I can't help looking over at the large four-poster bed. The room I shared with Luther was dark, small, and slightly seedy. But this is probably the nicest room I've ever been in. Mack catches me trailing my finger along the rim of the large standalone bathtub.

"I'll bring you back one day," he whispers in my ear. "I promise."

I turn and slip my hands inside his jacket. As we kiss, I close my eyes and lose myself in the feel of his mouth on mine.

When our lips part, I ask, "Has it been ten minutes? Please say it hasn't been ten minutes." Heat is trickling down my limbs.

Mack tweaks his index finger under my chin. "'Fraid so, Little Star." He straightens his jacket. "You're sure you're alright with this? There's time to back out."

"We have to," I tell him. "We're not backing out now. Not when we're so close."

MACK TAKES my hand and we sneak back out of the room, leaving our key in its slot so that anyone who looks at the computer system will think we're still inside. We won't be returning tonight, so it doesn't matter that we've locked ourselves out.

We take the stairwell to the third floor. We walk down a long corridor, and another, then finally arrive at the presidential suite. Two large gold doors are in front of us. Mack knocks purposefully then stands back, shielding me from view.

When the doors swing open, Annalise is wearing the same black dress and red lipstick, but a concerned expression contorts her face. She looks at Mack, then at me, then ushers us inside.

"Are we alone?" Mack asks, not stopping for pleasantries.

"Of course." Annalise smiles at him. For a moment, she

just looks at him. The softness in her eyes makes my skin burn with irritation. Can't she tell I'm the only one who should be looking at him like that? "Mack? Is this who I think it is?" she says quietly.

Mack puts his arm around my waist and nudges me forward. Closing my eyes, I unwind the masking spell in my mind. I feel it drop, feel my skin relax and the tingling sensation fade. When I open my eyes again, Annalise's mouth is hanging slightly open. She takes a step back and smooths her hands over her hips then flexes them at her sides like she's not quite sure what to do with them. "Oh, my," she says, her eyes landing on Mack's hand, which is still firmly on my waist. "Mack, what have you gotten yourself into?"

"We need your help." Mack doesn't waste any time and he doesn't take his arm from around me. With his free hand, he pulls out his cell phone and turns the screen to show Annalise the test results that Nico stole from the hospital. "You remember The Phoenix Prophecy, Annalise?" Mack asks as she studies the phone.

"Of course, I remember it." She tilts her head to the side.

"Nova is The Phoenix." Mack is unwavering in his conviction. "She was born human, but is becoming a fire witch. A powerful one. The tests clearly show that her DNA is changing."

Annalise bites her lower lip, then takes a step back. "Even if that's true," she says slowly, fixing a piercing stare on me. "She killed a human. With magick!"

Mack is about to defend me, but I raise my palm at him and move away, causing his arm to slip free. "Johnny was my ex-boyfriend. For years, he tortured me. Physically and emotionally. He made my life a living hell."

Annalise draws in a tight breath. "I'm sorry for what you went through," she says, "but the fact remains, you were caught on camera using magick to take his life. So, I'm not sure it matters whether you're human, or a witch, or an alien. You broke the pact."

A lead weight settles in my stomach. Clearly, this woman has no interest in helping us. "Mack, we're wasting our time." I tug his arm. "We should get out of here. Luther was right."

"Luther?" Annalise chuckles a little. "Well, the two of us never did see eye-to-eye."

"Annalise, please." Mack puts his hand on her elbow. "You know me. You know I wouldn't be here if I didn't need your help."

"I do know that," she says tightly. "But I honestly don't know how I *can* help." She puts her smooth palm on Mack's shoulder and adds, "You know I'd do anything to help you, Mack, if I could. But—"

"Annalise, you believe in the prophecy. I know you do." Frustration laces Mack's voice; he's losing his patience. I can sense it in the way the air around him changes. It's vibrating. "This isn't just about saving Nova from jail; it's about saving the world from what's about to happen." He starts to pace up and down. "You *can* help us. You can get the Bureau off our backs, so we can concentrate on stopping the League from unleashing hell on Earth."

Annalise screws her eyes shut. "Mack, that's a little dramatic—"

"No," he tells her, "it isn't." He dips his head to catch her eyes. "What's going on here, Annalise? Did you tell Tom to stab me in the back, or was that his own idea?"

For a moment, Annalise simply stares at Mack. Then she stalks over to the couch and sits down. "Would you pour us a drink?" she asks, gesturing to the drink cabinet in the corner of the room.

Mack obliges, pouring us each a whiskey. I simply cradle mine while Annalise takes a large drink from hers. "Mack? Nova? Sit down, please." Her voice is tight and a little shaky.

We perch in armchairs opposite her.

She taps her long fingernails on her glass. "I've long suspected that the Bureau was infiltrated by members of H.E.L. There is a lot going on behind the scenes. Things I can't explain to you right now." She exhales slowly but forcefully. "But I promise you, if I could have stopped Tom and his agents from attacking The Hollow, I would have."

Mack studies her face, clearly not quite sure how to react to what she's saying. "Annalise, you're about as high up as it gets. Are you telling me you have no power? There's nothing you can do to help us?"

Annalise wraps her arms around her stomach. She nods at Mack's phone then takes her own from a small table beside the couch. "Bluetooth me those test results. I'll see what I can do."

For a moment, there's a quivering silence. Then Mack shakes his head. "I'm sorry, that's not good enough. We're talking about the end of the world here, Annalise. Not just one person." He glances at me. "Not just one girl."

"But this *girl* is the real reason you're here, though, isn't she?" Annalise fires back. An unmistakable hint of jealousy laces her tone. "You're here because you're trying to protect her?"

Mack's jaw twitches.

Before he can answer her, I interrupt. "Mack brought me here because he trusts you." I stand up and walk over to the window. Staring down at the twinkling city lights, I shake my head. "I didn't ask for this. Mack didn't either. But somehow, we've been thrown together. He believes in the prophecy. At first, I didn't know what to believe. But now, having seen what I've seen?" A cold shiver runs through me. I push it away and blink some fire into my palm. "I feel the power inside me growing. Every minute. Every hour. There's a heat in my soul that won't subside." I look at Annalise, meeting her eyes through the dancing flames. "The League wants me dead. The reason they want me dead is because they believe I can stop them from raising the underworld. Those are facts. Cold, hard facts."

Annalise is watching me carefully. I move the flames from one palm to the other, then separate them into tiny balls of fire and send them spinning in a circle.

"If the Bureau won't help us fight the League, the least they can do is leave us alone." I snuff out the flames and lean back against the window ledge. "The least they can do is give us the chance to win."

Mack's eyes soften as he watches me. His approving gaze brings a flutter of butterflies to my stomach.

"We can't help you fight the League," Annalise says stiffly. She pauses, sucking in her breath as she turns to me. "Your fireworks are very lovely, Nova. But if you're going to win this fight, like you say you are, you'll need more. *Much* more." She puts down her glass. "I believe there is someone who can help you with that."

I glance at Mack. He takes a long, slow sip of his drink.

"The original prophecy was cast by a seer from the Foresight Commune." Annalise stands, walks to the small console table near the minibar, and scribbles something on a complimentary notepad. "I believe she knows more than she shared with us." She passes Mack the piece of paper. His eyes narrow as he reads it.

When he looks up, he asks, "This is the name of the seer? The seer who was first sent the prophecy?"

"Yes," Annalise replies. Something passes between them that I can't catch hold of or name. A shared moment. A shared… something.

Mack scrunches the paper in his fist and puts it into his pocket. "You think she can help us stop the League?"

"I think she can help you tap into Nova's power." Annalise

presses her lips together into a thin line. "In the meantime," she says, standing up and moving toward the door, "I will do what I can to keep my agents away from Nova." She puts her hand on the doorknob. "But I can't make you any promises, Mack. Like I said, the situation here is fragile."

Taking my arm, Mack ushers me to the door.

"You should go now. I've been away from the party long enough." She adjusts her skirt nervously then straightens up and smiles at us. Pressing a keycard into Mack's hand, she says, "This will get you out of the building. Basement exit is easiest. The doors are locked but the card will let you through them."

"Thank you." Mack takes the card then pulls her in for a quick embrace as I linger beside him. Seeing his arms around another woman sends a heavy knot of nausea to my stomach.

"Find the seer," Annalise says as she opens the door. "Find her and find the truth behind the prophecy. Then, maybe you'll find enough power to win your fight."

14

NOVA

We stand in silence beside one another. The elevator is descending slowly toward the basement of the hotel and the parking lot where we left the truck. I glance at Mack. His arms are folded, his brow furrowed like he's deep in thought.

The way Annalise hugged him as we left is replaying in my mind. *I'd do anything for you, Mack* is what she said. She'd do *anything* for him.

"Did you hope for more?" I ask him. "Did you hope she'd do more?"

Mack pushes his fingers through his hair. "Yes, but at least she gave us something. She's clearly in a difficult position. Especially if the Bureau has been infiltrated."

I nod slowly. There is a moment's silence then, before I can stop myself, fiery indignation surging in my belly, I hear myself saying, "Mack, did you and Annalise ever...? Were you more than work colleagues?"

Without turning to look at me, Mack rubs his beard. He sighs a little. "What do you mean?"

"You know what I mean." My voice is a little louder now.

"When you worked together, did you two…?"

Mack closes his eyes. "Nova, this isn't the time."

"I'd like to know." I'm trying to press down the cartwheels of fire in my stomach, but I can't. It's not working. "Because the way she looked at you, and the way she spoke to you—"

"Why would you ask me that?" Mack's voice isn't like it usually is. It's different. Like I've hurt him.

I search for words that won't make me sound like a jealous teenager. Quietly, I say, "Because she's stunning, and she's older than me, and the way she looked at you—"

I'm studying Mack's profile. His shoulders are moving heavily up and down as he breathes. "I know I'm being ridiculous," I say quietly. "I know there is so much more at stake right now, so much more I should be worrying about. And I know that you have a past. Of course, you do. You're fifty-two years old. You've probably slept with hundreds of women." I pause and suck in a tear-filled breath. "But maybe that's it. Maybe that's why it hurts so much to think of you fucking Annalise… because you won't fuck me. You said today that you'd never cross that line with me and—"

Before I can finish my sentence, Mack spins around and punches the big red button on the wall. The elevator jolts to a stop so hard I almost topple over.

Finally, he turns to look at me. "First of all," he says darkly, "I never fucked Annalise. Never wanted to." Mack takes hold of my wrist. His grip is firm and warm. "Second of all, I have not slept with hundreds of women. Not even close." His eyes flash amber. "Third of all…" He licks his lower lip. "Even if I had, nothing would compare to the way I feel when I'm around you." His jaw twitches. "The world is in danger of being swallowed up, and you're all I can think about." He moves closer. "You are the most beautiful woman I've ever seen in my life." Still holding my wrist, he inches us toward the wall and presses into me, his hips hard up against my pelvis. "The things you do to me..." He towers over me. "The way you make me feel... it's sinful, Nova. The things I want to do to you. The ways I want to make you come."

Liquid heat drips through my body. My legs are trembling. "Then why won't you fuck me?" I ask, almost pleading. "You hold back. All the time." I tug my arm, but he won't let go. A tear rolls down my cheek. "When we're alone, you'll only go so far. When we're with the others, you let them take the lead." I tug again. He still holds me tight. Looking up at him, through my heavy eye makeup, I meet his steely gaze. "Why won't you fuck me, Daddy?"

A low rumble comes from deep inside Mack's chest. It sends vibrations through my limbs. I'm breathing hard, my breasts pressed against him. I feel his erection against my leg. When I move to touch him, he grabs my other wrist too and holds me still. Meeting my eyes, he says, "Because I don't deserve to feel that good."

A jolt of sympathy hits my stomach. He doesn't *deserve* to feel good? He deserves everything. All of it!

"Then do it for me." I tip my chin up, fix my gaze on his. I lower my voice and raise up on my tiptoes. Into his ear, I whisper, "Fuck me, Daddy. Right now. Make me come. Show me how good you can make me feel. Show me how you can take care of me."

A flickering moment passes between us, then Mack pushes me away, letting go of my wrists. I'm about to yell at him, scream at him to stop punishing himself. Then I realize he's unfastening his belt.

Mack fixes his gaze on me. Slowly, purposefully, he wraps the belt around his hand.

Watching him, a shiver runs down my spine.

He studies me for a moment, his breath rising and falling in his chest. When he finally stalks toward me, heat rushes to my core.

"You want me to let loose?" he growls, towering over me, running the cool leather of his belt up my arm. "You want to see the real Mack?"

I can't speak. I just nod, moistening my lower lip as his belt-wrapped hand reaches my throat and draws a slow line across it.

"Then turn around," Mack whispers.

My heart thundering in my chest, I do as he says. When I'm facing the wall, he presses against my back and pushes me hard, caging me in with his body.

"Stay there," he barks. "Hands on the wall."

I raise my palms and press them flat against the side of the elevator. Anticipation tingles on my skin. Then his heat disappears. I feel him move away from me and hear his footsteps as he

paces back and forth—like he's deciding whether to lecture me or punish me.

When he stops pacing, without speaking, he tucks his fingers under the straps of my emerald green dress and—just like that—snaps them.

The fabric hangs loose, but still covers my chest. Mack curls over my body from behind, trails his index finger across my collar bones, traces the lines of Kole's tattoo, feeling the raised flesh beneath it. For a second, he hesitates. As if he's reminding himself that I'm vulnerable, that someone did horrible things to me once, and that he should *not* give in to temptation.

When I sway back toward him, turning my head and parting my lips, he understands I want him to kiss me.

With his belt still wrapped around his hand, he tucks his fingers under my chin and holds my face still. He steals a kiss, hungry and searching. I moan into his mouth.

Brushing my curled hair over my shoulders, he stops

kissing me and stands back. He runs his hands down my sides, releasing an appreciative sigh.

Finally, he returns to my dress. After easing it down over my breasts, he moves his expert hands to my back and unclips my strapless bra. It falls to the floor. I wait for him to turn me around and put his mouth on me, but he doesn't. Instead, he hitches up the skirt of my dress and finds my panties. He bends down as he rolls them toward my ankles, then gently lifts each of my feet and helps me step out of them.

Pressing his large heavy chest against my back, he whispers into my ear, "Who do you belong to?" His voice lands like melted chocolate on my skin.

"You," I breathe.

"Who do you belong to?" he repeats, slamming my hands back onto the wall as I attempt to turn around and face him.

My heart hammers against my ribs. Fuck, I need this. Teasing him felt good. Tying him up and making him writhe beneath me made me feel all kinds of powerful. But, in a strange way, letting him take control gives me power too. "I belong to you, Daddy."

Mack hums darkly, planting a rough kiss on my bare shoulder. "Now, be a good girl and stay quiet." He reaches around and puts a finger into my mouth. As I suck it, he asks, "Can you do that for me, Nova?"

I nod, desperate for him to touch me. Desperate for his praise to wash over me again.

"Can you stay quiet while I make you come? Because if someone catches us in here, we'll be in trouble. Big trouble."

I nod again, but already—as his hands find my nipples—it's almost impossible to remain silent. When a small mewing sound escapes my lips, Mack stops, takes his hands away, and stands back.

He puts his hand around my throat and flexes his fingers.

Before I can promise him I'll do better next time, he's shoved my panties into my mouth. "Maybe now you'll stay quiet?" he asks, tilting my head and kissing my forehead tenderly.

But it still doesn't work. I'm so turned on it's like I'm on fire. I wait for him with fizzing anticipation. When he puts his hand between my legs and traces a long, knowing finger along my folds, I shudder and moan through the gag.

Mack takes his hand away. "Naughty girl," he sighs. Then he reaches round me and punches the red button on the elevator wall.

We're moving again. I'm shaking. My dress is broken, my breasts are exposed, and I have no idea if I'm allowed to move now or not. Arousal hums on my skin. As the elevator moves down through the floors, I pull my panties from my mouth and pick up my bra while Mack puts his belt back on.

I've just managed to haul my dress up and cover myself when the elevator stops.

Putting his hand on the small of my back, without looking at me, Mack leads me down an empty corridor toward the parking lot. He swipes the card Annalise gave us, letting us out, and heads for the truck.

We're barely inside when he pushes his seat back and pulls me across his lap. I start fumbling with his belt, but he says, "No. Move this way. Ass in the air."

My core pulses. I slide across his lap and brace my hands on the door. Slowly, Mack pulls my dress up. He smooths his hands over my cheeks, then pulls his arm back and slaps me hard.

The sound of the slap makes me jump. Pain moves like a lightning rod from my ass to my pussy. I squirm and bite my lower lip. Again, Mack spanks me. Then again, and again. Each time, he rubs my skin afterward, soothing the sore spot as he grows harder beneath me.

"Now, can you be quiet?" he asks, leaning down to whisper in my ear.

I nod, silently.

"Can you come quickly for me? Quickly and quietly so we're not caught?"

"Yes, Daddy," I whisper, so turned on I feel like I might come at the slightest contact between his fingers and my cunt.

Without speaking, he helps me sit up and lifts me onto his lap. He reaches down and unzips his pants. I slide back on his knees to admire his impressive length. Seeing him like this, protruding from his smart black dress pants, every inch the gentleman, makes my mouth water.

I smile and wrap both hands around his cock, then rub my thumbs over its tip. Mack closes his eyes and rests his head back. Pleasure softens his features.

I rise up on my knees and position him beneath me. Mack catches my face with his hands and kisses me. He runs his hands over my shoulders, pulling my dress back down. As he brushes his large thumbs over my hard pink buds, I whisper, "Will you fuck me now, Mack?"

He strokes my hair from my face. Before he's had chance to say yes, I drop down hard and brace my hand on the roof of the truck as he impales me.

He lets out a groan and grabs my hips. "Nova…"

"I thought we had to be quiet," I whisper in his ear.

"You're so wet," he mutters. "You're such a good girl. So wet and ready for me."

"Fuck me, Daddy," I whisper in his ear. "Please, don't stop now."

So, he does. He thrusts up into me. He claws at my back. He pulls my hair. Sweat glistens on his forehead. I lean back, grinding into him. He finds my clit and massages it fast, urgent, determined.

As my orgasm rolls through me, I yell and fall forward, clutching the back of his head, holding him to my chest.

Mack clings onto me as if he's afraid I'll slip away from him. When he comes, his body tenses beneath me. He holds me tighter, and tighter, barely breathing. Then he shudders, panting, kissing my chest and my neck.

The truck is stiflingly hot. Mack rolls down the window, and some sparks escape, fluttering into the darkness of the parking lot. He looks up at me, cups my face, strokes my damp hair from my cheeks.

"Are you glad you gave in?" I ask, weaving my fingers between the buttons of his shirt so I can touch his bare chest.

Mack shakes his head. He pushes his fingers through his hair. "Nova…"

"Are you glad?" I meet his eyes. "Did the world end? Is everything terrible now?" I laugh a little and take his hand so I can kiss his knuckles.

He sighs and closes his eyes. "Yes," he whispers, "I'm glad but also, yes, everything is terrible now."

My breath catches in my chest. Tears bite at my throat. I'm too high from my orgasm to cope with him telling me he regrets what just happened. I inhale sharply, but Mack wraps his big arms around me and pulls me closer.

"Everything is terrible now because I have to admit I'm in love with you."

I freeze, stiff against him.

"I don't deserve to be in love with you." He strokes my back. "I haven't loved anyone for a long, long time." His lips brush against my shoulder. "The people I love get hurt. I'm no good. You don't need me. You have the others."

I pull back so he has to look at me. "Stop it." I stroke my fingers over his forehead then through his hair. I stare into his eyes. "Stop saying that." I kiss the bridge of his nose. "I do need you. I need all of you." His beard scratches against my chest as he kisses my throat. I hold him close, then I whisper. "It's not your fault she died, Rhone."

Hearing me say his real name, Mack sucks in a deep breath. He tries to look away from me, but I bring his face back.

"It's not your fault," I tell him again. "She wouldn't want you to be alone. If she loved you the way I love you, she wouldn't want you to be sad."

Mack nuzzles into my neck, kisses my chest, sighs against me.

"Please don't keep me at a distance," I whisper. "Because I love you too, Daddy. And I know you won't hurt me."

Mack lifts his head, stares into my eyes, then he starts to smile. Not a happy smile, a relieved smile.

I wriggle in his lap. I run my hands up his shirt and tweak his bowtie. "No more holding back. Okay?"

Gently, Mack tugs my dress back up to cover my breasts. He rubs my upper arms, then takes his jacket off and wraps it around my shoulders. "Okay," he says. "Okay, Nova."

15

KOLE

It's late. Luther has downed half a whiskey bottle waiting for Nova and Mack to return, and Sam's been out in the woods so long I'm starting to worry where he got to. Opposite me, Tanner sighs and shoves his coffee mug across the table. "Fuck," he says. "Shouldn't they be back by now?"

"It's not midnight yet. Give them a chance." I sit back in my chair. Every time I look across the living room, I see the last time the three of us were together. When we were playing with each other like there was nothing else to think about. When I hung her upside down and buried my face between her thighs. Before I lost it and sunk my teeth into her neck.

I must have been licking my teeth because Tanner says, "You still want her?"

I inhale slowly and lean onto my elbows. "When I'm near her, I want *her*." I steeple my fingers together. "I don't think about..." I pause.

"Her blood?" Tanner finishes for me.

I nod. "That happens when we fuck. When she comes. When she melts around me… it's intoxicating."

Tanner adjusts himself under the table. Before Nova came into our lives, we'd have blown off steam together at a time like this. Now, it feels wrong doing it without her. Like she was the missing piece we needed to complete us.

On the couch, Luther starts to snore and drops his whiskey glass from his hand. "Shit," Tanner says, "what are we going to do about him? He's driving himself crazy."

"Not much we can do. He needs to talk to Nova."

"I think he did a little more than that." Tanner picks up a handful of potato chips and starts crunching on them loudly. He watches my face for my reaction.

"What?"

"This morning. I sensed something between those two. Something that wasn't there before." He shrugs. "Could be wrong, but didn't you wonder how the bathroom mirror got broken?"

Something bubbles deep in my chest. Before I realize what I'm doing, I'm shoving my chair back so hard it clatters to the floor and striding to the couch. Tanner calls my name, but I ignore him. I grab Luther and throw him to the floor. He wakes up, scrambling to his feet.

"What the fuck, Kole?"

"You fucked her?" I slam my hand around his throat and squeeze. "After everything we said, you fucked her?"

Luther starts to cough. He could burn my hands off his throat, but he doesn't. Tanner watches us. After several long moments, I let go and shake my arms at my sides. "Fuck, Luther, why?"

"Because you're right!" Luther yells so loudly the walls of the cabin rattle. "You're right. I can't stop thinking about her. I can't get her out of my head." He taps his forehead hard with his index finger. "She's in here, twenty-four-seven. Even when I was inside her, it felt like it wasn't enough." He laughs loudly and reaches for the whiskey bottle.

I swipe it from his hands. The anger beating in my ribcage is subsiding. "So, then why are you torturing yourself?"

Luther opens his mouth to answer me, but no sound comes out.

Stepping between us, Tanner says, "Because he's fucked up, Kole. Just like the rest of us. He's got demons living in his head the same as you and me. Only his demons come in the shape of humans, so the fact he's falling for one is a head-fuck." He looks at Luther. "That about sum it up?"

Grimacing, rubbing his palm over his shaved head, Luther nods. "Just about."

Watching my friend's face crumple, I sink to the couch and lean onto my thighs. "Shit, man."

"Yeah. Shit." Luther sits opposite me on the coffee table. After a few seconds, he meets my eyes. "I won't hurt her," he says. "I might be handling this all kinds of wrong, but I won't hurt her."

I shake my head at him then hand Tanner the bottle. "Ditch this," I tell him. "Down the sink. It's making things worse."

Luther looks like he's about to object but decides against it.

"I'll make more coffee." Tanner takes the bottle to the kitchen and puts the kettle on the stove.

When he returns with three mugs of terribly made coffee, he sits next to Luther. "So," he says, "how'd it happen?"

Luther glances at me.

"Might as well tell us," I say. "I've got the visual anyway."

Shaking his head, Luther stares down into his mug. "She caught me," he says, a pained expression on his face.

"Caught you?" Tanner asks, a little too intrigued.

Luther groans and buries his face in his palm. "Jerking off with her underwear in my face."

I nearly spit my coffee out.

Tanner lets out a guffaw and slaps his thigh.

"Yeah, real fucking funny," Luther says.

"But she didn't call you a pervert and walk out." Tanner adds.

"No." Luther glances toward the bathroom. "She didn't."

"Then, for fuck's sake, talk to her properly." Tanner thumps Luther on the shoulder.

"Easy for the empath to say." I raise my eyebrows to lighten the mood. "We're not all such fluent communicators."

"You can say that again." Luther meets my eyes. Before he can say anything else I gesture to his coffee.

"Drink. You might have more luck figuring this out if you're sober."

SAM

S itting inside and waiting for Nova to return wasn't an option. My skin was crawling with nerves. Minutes felt like hours, so I left the guys to it, and escaped outside.

I barely made it down the steps out front before shifting.

Being in the forest is intoxicating enough in human form, but when I shift... holy hell it feels good.

My senses are in overdrive. I race into the darkness and hurtle through the undergrowth like an excited pup. I roll on my back, feel leaves and twigs scrunch beneath me, sniff every fucking thing I can find to sniff, pee on several tree trunks.

On four legs, I make it to the very edge of the mask the guys created in no time and decide to trace the perimeter. I can smell each of them; their scent lingers in the air, the ground, the leaves. Nova's is strongest. It brings saliva to my mouth and makes me growl protectively. I know Polar Daddy will take care of her, but I also know I've lived too much of my life not being by her side.

For so long, I thought I was crazy to believe she was still

alive. To feel like she was still out there somewhere waiting for me. The night she appeared in the club, everything slotted into place. I realized I wasn't simply damaged from being locked up all those years; I was right. She was there all along.

When I reach the lake, I stop and stare into the water at my reflection. Like our clothes, wolves' scars shift with us. My fur covers some of the marks, but the deeper ones are still visible. If my fur was orange, I'd look more like a tiger than a wolf—jagged lines creating a strange pattern on my back, causing my fur to rest in the wrong direction so I look like I've been wet and somehow dried the wrong way up.

I'm taking a drink, lapping cool clear water into my dry throat, when I hear something.

A twig snaps. Not a small snap from a mouse or a rabbit —a loud snap. Something bigger. I sniff the air. *Wolf.*

Bolting through the trees, I follow the scent. A wolf in the forest can't be good news. Either Madame's changed her mind and sent my brothers to bring me back, or H.E.L. has sent its wolfpack after Nova.

I slow my pace as the smell grows stronger, lower my body to the ground, pad quietly through the trees. In front of me, the mask shimmers as moonlight bounces off it. I stay in the shadow and watch.

From the darkness, a black wolf appears. He has piercing eyes, and his frame is large but slender. I tilt my head to the side. The wolf is sniffing the ground. It knows the mask is there, and that it can't pass through.

Looking up, it stares into the shadows toward me. It can sense me, even though it can't see me.

Knowing I'm hidden by the mask, I pad toward the black wolf. It sits down on its haunches and doesn't move. Like it's waiting for me, it just sits there. Stock still. Staring at me but not seeing me.

Are you Sam? A voice enters my head with such force I almost cry out.

How do you know me? I reply, even though I have no idea how I'm doing it.

Can I see you? the voice asks.

Even though everything inside me tells me it's a bad idea, I answer, *Yes.*

In just two quick strides, I'm on the other side of the mask. The black wolf blinks at me. It takes me in, then its gaze flickers to my paw. I look down. It's noticed my birthmark. The one that becomes a small white splash of fur when I shift.

You're Sam, the wolf says. A statement not a question.

I cock my head to the side, trying to understand how he's talking to me like this because I've *never* communicated in wolf form before. Ever. Back in *Spine*, there was only deafening silence when my brothers and I shifted. Yet, somehow, this black wolf can place its words in my head?

Like a dog offering a human its paw, the black wolf lifts its foot. We are inches away from one another now. I've barely managed to process the fact I'm looking at a white splash of fur that's almost identical to mine when the black wolf shudders. Its limbs blur. It yowls quietly. In a flurry of movement, the wolf shifts back into its human form.

A man has appeared in front of me. Young. My age. Dark floppy hair, broad shoulders, but—like his wolf counterpart —a slight frame. He's wearing a black t-shirt and gray jeans, but he's barefoot.

Crouching down, he swipes his fingers through his hair and stares at me. "You're Sam," he repeats. Out loud this time.

I try to ask his name, but the question bounces back into my own head and sends a jolt of pain through my skull.

"Only works wolf-to-wolf," he says, tapping his temple with his forefinger.

Reluctantly, I shift back. He watches as I become myself again. When we both raise up to our full heights, he looks down at my wrist. I turn it up to face the night sky.

He steps forward. Without touching me, he extends his arm and turns his wrist upward too. His birthmark is the same as mine. On the opposite wrist, but the same. A splash of dark skin that looks like a bird.

Our eyes meet. "Who are you?" I whisper.

"I'm your brother," he replies.

* * *

FOR A LONG MOMENT, neither of us speaks. Finally, I cross my arms and take several steps back. "I don't have a brother," I snarl, trying not to notice how eerily similar we look. I have more muscle than him—years of dancing in *Spine* took care of that—but we are the same height. Our hair is alike, our eyes, our noses.

I shake my head. "I don't have a brother," I repeat.

"I thought so, too," he replies. "My whole life I thought so, too. Until my mother finally told me the truth."

"Who is your mother?" I ask.

He screws his eyes shut. "It's complicated," he says. When he opens his eyes, he looks past me into the trees. "But I actually didn't come here for you." His expression changes. "I had no idea she'd found you."

"Nova?" Her name is like fire on my tongue.

"Yes. I came for Nova."

Hearing her name on his lips, the pieces suddenly slot into place. Nova's only had contact with one werewolf other than me. A werewolf who *pretended* to be me and wormed himself into her life. "You're Nico?" I slam my hand around his throat before he has the chance to answer me. "You dare come here? After what you did?" With my free hand, I grab his arm and yank it up toward his face. Jerking my eyes from his face to the obviously fake birthmark on his wrist, I spit, "You expect me to believe this shit? You expect me to buy that you're my brother when I know the pack of lies you told her?"

"Please," Nico goes limp in my grasp. His voice is hoarse, his face reddening in the moonlight. "Just let me see her. I can help her. I came here to help."

As Nico starts to shift beneath my fingers, I shift too. I lunge for his throat, sink my teeth into his shoulder, then pin him to the ground with my own body. He doesn't fight me, just lays there shivering.

Tipping my head up toward the moon, energy surges up my throat and I howl so loudly the trees shake.

NOVA

"**B**efore we go back to the cabin, there's something I need to tell you." Mack has stopped the truck in the turnout and is reaching for the piece of paper in his pocket. "The name Annalise gave us…"

I tilt my head to read it. "Thessaly Trajan?" My forehead creases. "Why does that sound familiar?"

Mack brushes his thumb over Annalise's looped handwriting. "Because Thessaly Trajan is Kole's mother."

"Trajan?" I blink at the name. Mack's words don't quite compute. "Kole has a mother?" is what leaves my mouth, which is utterly stupid; of course, he has a mother. I just can't picture her. What kind of woman gives birth to a mage like Kole?

"He was raised in the Foresight Commune." Mack opens the truck door and walks around to the passenger side to help me down. "They're a group of powerful seers, all from ancient magick bloodlines."

"That's why Kole is so powerful?"

Mack nods, putting his arm around my waist as we start back toward the cabin.

"But if his mother was the first to access the prophecy—"

"She was *sent* the prophecy, it's different." Mack turns to me. He's using his professor voice again, which always makes me feel a little tingly. "Prophecies are not common. When they do occur, they're sent to a seer. Usually, a pureblood like Thessaly or Kole."

"Sent by who?"

Mack laughs a little and tilts his head. "That's a question for a theologist. Some believe it's a god. Some believe it's fate. Others believe it's magickal forces we can't possibly comprehend."

"What do you believe?"

"I believe it's best to focus on what we know for sure, which is that when prophecies are sent, the seer who receives them is duty-bound to record them in some way. These days, all seers must pass their prophecies to the Bureau. But for a long time, they were just kept on scrolls or in crystals."

"And then others can *access* them?" I ask, my brain struggling to keep up.

"Exactly, but only powerful seers can access prophecies that have been received by others."

I frown and rub my temples. "So, Kole accessed his mother's prophecy. But he never knew she was the seer who received it?"

Mack nods. "Seems that way, yes."

"Would she have known? That he was involved?" Those familiar words *fated to five* echo in my head. "Would she have known he was part of it?"

"I guess that's what we're going to find out," Mack says. "If we can persuade Kole to take us to Foresight."

We're almost at the cabin when I catch Mack's arm. "You're sure we can trust Annalise?"

"Nova…" His tone is on the verge of being a warning.

"I'm not jealous of her anymore, I promise." I squeeze his

butt playfully. "I'm just asking if you're sure we can trust her. Because if we're going to follow her advice—"

"I'm sure." Mack slides his hand to the back of my neck. "I wouldn't have put you in danger tonight if I wasn't one hundred percent certain." He brushes his lips across my forehead. "I would never put you in danger, Nova."

I slot my hand into his and keep hold of it as we approach the cabin.

As if they sensed us, the others are waiting on the veranda. I let go of Mack and fall into the middle of Tanner and Kole.

Little Star. Kole's voice rushes through me. *You're home.* "What happened?" he asks out loud, assessing the broken straps on my dress.

"I'm okay," I tell him, then glance at Mack.

"Inside," Mack says. "Let's talk inside."

Looking around the living room, it's pretty obvious the guys spent the last few hours eating and drinking to pass the time. The place is a mess. Tanner moves to the couch and pulls me onto his lap. Almost instantly, his muscles tense. He can feel the trepidation in my belly. "Nova?" he whispers. "What happened?"

I squeeze his hand. "Listen to Mack," I tell him quietly.

Before he sits down, Mack asks, "Where's Sam?"

"Out for a run," Tanner replies. "He should be back soon."

Mack stands by the window and takes his piece of paper from his pocket. "Okay. We can catch Sam up later. Long story short, Annalise can't do much to help us. Something's going on at the Bureau. She thinks they've been infiltrated by H.E.L. She said she'd do her best to get her agents off our back, but aside from that, all she could do was give us the name of the seer who first accessed The Phoenix Prophecy. She said perhaps this witch will be able to help Nova understand her power and what we have to do to defeat Ragnor."

Amazed at his succinct explanation, I look at the others. Luther, Tanner, and Kole are all nodding. "You have the name of the original seer?" Kole asks, moving purposefully toward Mack. "That's invaluable. If we can speak to the witch —" He stops when he notices the strange expression on Mack's face.

Without saying any more, Mack hands Kole the piece of paper.

Kole's eyes graze the words. His jaw tenses. His face darkens. "This is the name you were given?"

Mack puts a brotherly hand on Kole's shoulder. "Annalise said the seer was from the Foresight Commune." He taps the paper. "She said this is the name of the seer who was sent The Phoenix Prophecy."

"Do you know who this is?" Kole's voice is like gravel.

"I believe," says Mack gently, "it's your mother."

There's a moment of quivering silence in which no one speaks. Luther breaks ranks first. "Your mother?" He moves to Kole's elbow and stares at Annalise's handwriting.

"Unless there's another Thessaly Trajan living in the Foresight Commune," Kole says, his fist tightening around his mother's name.

"Shit," breathes Tanner, sliding me from his lap so he can stand next to Kole.

If a million questions were burning in my head when Mack told me, a million more must be racing through Kole's. He steps away from us. Pulling his hair loose from its tie, as if it might help him think straight, he says, "She never told me. Never even mentioned it."

"Perhaps she didn't know it involved you," Tanner offers.

Kole scoffs at that. "Of course, she knew. She had to have known."

"You haven't seen her for a long time, Kole. Things changed for you in the last five years. Maybe—"

"I see her every year." Kole's eyes snap toward Tanner's.

Something passes between them. Tanner looks confused. "Every year? I thought...?"

Kole's lips tighten. "I didn't tell you because..." He shakes his head. It makes his hair move in waves over his shoulders. "That doesn't matter now. What matters is you're saying we have to visit my mother?" He's looking at Mack.

"I think so," Mack says. "We can't do anymore to get the Bureau off our back, but we do need to know more about Nova's power. How to harness it. How she's supposed to win this fight. Your mother might be able to help."

Placing a gentle hand on Kole's elbow, I tell him, "Kole, if it's going to be too hard, we don't have to go."

Kole stares down at me. I can't read his expression. Looking at the others, he barks, "We'll leave tomorrow at sundown. There's a sleeper cargo train that passes through the Fore Valley. It's how I get to the Commune unseen."

I don't ask him why he has to travel unseen when he's visiting his family, just nod. Tanner is about to say something else when Mack raises his hand.

"Quiet," he says. "Do you hear that?"

We all stop talking.

Mack's eyes flash amber. "It sounded like a wolf."

TANNER

Nova is the first to bolt for the door, Mack's jacket falling from her shoulder as she runs. Luther pulls her out of the way and speeds past her. Down the steps, into the trees. He's always been the fastest among us and disappears leaving a trail of sparks on the ground beneath him.

Kole and I up front, Mack keeping pace with Nova, we follow Luther's path.

When we find Luther, he's standing just inside the mask, staring out at two wolves. The smaller, darker one is pinned to the ground. A larger one, with scars in its fur, has its jaw around the black one's neck.

When I notice the flash of white on the black one's foot, I realize who Sam has trapped.

"Fucking Nico," I growl, striding through the mask, exposing myself without giving a shit.

"Nico?" Luther follows at my elbow. When he sees us, Sam lets go of Nico's neck and jumps back, panting. He shifts back to himself and pulls Nova to him as she rushes forward.

Inching her back, away from the black wolf on the floor,

Sam snaps his eyes to me and snarls, "He says he's here for Nova."

Together, Luther and I reach for the wolf, but he shifts before we can catch hold of him. Standing in front of us as Nico, he raises his palms. He's shaking—he shifted too fast— and the color has drained from his face. "Wait," he stammers. "Please, wait."

But Luther doesn't wait, he slams a restraint spell onto Nico's wrists and ankles, sending him to the ground. On his knees, Nico searches for Nova.

Emotions swirl around her, but I can't latch onto them. Her eyes darting from Sam to Nico, she inches forward. Mack looks about to move in front of her when she raises her palm to stop him.

"What do you want, Nico?" she spits, staring down at him, managing to look both hot as hell with her dress half falling off and seriously intimidating at the same time. "Why are you here?"

Pride swells in my stomach. Our girl is fucking fierce when she wants to be. The others hang back too, sensing that she needs to be the one to dish it out if an ass-kicking is going to happen.

"I have information." Nico's voice is hoarse and shaky. "About Ragnor."

Nova narrows her eyes at him. "Ragnor?"

"He's the head of the League," Nico says.

"We know who he is," I cut in. "No thanks to you."

"Everything I did," Nico stutters, "it was because of him. Because he made me."

"You spineless piece of shit," Luther spits. "He *made* you?"

Nico closes his eyes and sighs deeply. Something washes over him: sorrow, guilt, remorse.

Turning to me, Nova asks, "Tanner, is he telling the truth?"

"We know how good he is at shielding his thoughts. I can't be sure what I'm feeling is real."

"I'm not hiding anything," Nico says. "Is there a spell you can do to test me? If there is, do it." He is practically begging. Desperation hums on his skin, but I wouldn't trust this wolf as far as I could throw him. "I swear. I'm here to help you, Nova. I'm here to make amends."

"Bullshit," Kole spits, flexing his fingers. His eyes flash green. The trees around us creak. Branches bend and twist and snake toward Nico like tendrils.

As one curls around Nico's throat, Nova says, "Stop, Kole. Release his ankle ties. Bring him inside."

"Inside?" Kole is still staring at Nico.

"If he has information, we should hear him out." Nova puts her hand on his arm.

For a moment, the branches continue to tighten around Nico's throat. Then Kole releases the tension in his palms, and they stop.

"Seriously? You're bringing him inside?" Luther asks incredulously.

"He has no magick," Kole replies. "What can he do to us?"

"Bring his friends here?" Luther's eyes flash with anger.

"If he wanted to do that, he could have." Nova looks around the group, adjusting her dress as she speaks. "If Nico found us and wanted to hurt me, or help Ragnor to hurt me, why would he bother trying to sneak past the mask? We're all out here in the open right now. No one has come. We're still alone."

"She's right." I don't mean about Nico; I mean about being out here, completely exposed. "Let's get him inside and talk."

"Search him first," Luther says. "At least search the fucker."

Nodding, Mack pats Nico down then casts a quick and dirty revealing spell. It envelops him in a soft white light. We watch, waiting for it to change color and show us he's a werewolf-shaped bomb or a life-sized listening device. When the light remains white, Luther reluctantly snaps the ankle spell, and Kole marches Nico through the mask toward the cabin.

With the others up ahead, I hang back with Nova and Sam. She rubs his back. "Are you alright? How did you find him?"

"I sensed him," Sam replies. Confusion comes off him in clouds. He's barely able to think straight. Sam stumbles on his words. "He said he's my brother."

"He said what?" My forehead creases into a frown. I'm picturing the birthmark. The one I thought was fake.

Nova is looking at Sam's wrist, clearly thinking the same thing. "Could that be possible?" she asks me.

I press my lips together, trying to reel back through the timeline of Sam's life that we learned from Sarah. "I mean, it's not *impossible*," I say.

Sam looks like he might throw up.

"But I think we should hold back on trusting Nico until we've heard his story." I pat Sam's back. "So far, I'm not convinced."

"Right." Sam looks up at the cabin. He draws in a deep breath. "Then let's go hear the fucker out."

INSIDE, Kole and Mack toss Nico onto the couch. Nova sits on the coffee table in front of him, and we crowd around her in an arch. I'm just about ready to waterboard this fucker to get the truth out of him, but clearly, she wants to try a different approach.

"Nova…" Nico meets her eyes, tugging a little against his restraints.

Calmly, she shakes her head at him. "No small talk. Just tell me what you came here to say."

Nico's gaze darts from Nova to Sam. His jaw twitches before he sucks in a deep breath. "Ragnor is my father."

Sam's eyes widen. He rubs his arms and takes a step back. "Your father?" he mutters.

Nico nods fervently. "He's *our* father," he says. "But I didn't know anything about you until a few days ago."

Nova crosses her arms impatiently, as we are all waiting for the rest of the story.

Stumbling a little over his words, Nico continues, "Ragnor never wanted anything to do with me. He made me believe that if I proved myself—if I did what he asked time and again—eventually he'd welcome me. But it was all a lie." He hangs his head. Shame vibrates on his skin. "I was raised to be a spy. A mole. A pawn for H.E.L. to use in their games." He meets Nova's gaze. "I had no idea what he was going to ask me to do that night—the night they pulled me up on stage and made me pretend to be Sam." He swallows hard. "He had Eve burn the scars into my chest, told me all I had to do was say I was this guy named Sam. Get you to believe I was your brother. That's it. Then, when you guys came and pulled us out..." Nico looks around at the rest of us, "I was told to stay close. Watch. Listen."

"They faked that too?" Sam steps forward and sits down next to Nova. He's pointing at Nico's wrist. "The birthmark?"

Nico shakes his head. A wry smile crosses his lips. "No. This is real." He looks pleadingly into Sam's eyes. "I really am your brother." Then he looks at Nova. "Which I guess, in a way, means—" He stops when Nova narrows her eyes at him, disgust swimming in her face.

"If Ragnor is your father," Kole's gruff voice interrupts, "who is your mother?"

"I'm not sure I can tell you that," Nico mutters.

"Why?"

"Because you hate her, and it'll make you hate me even more. But I love her, and I don't want her dragged into this."

As Kole's eyes widen, I know exactly what he's going to say. The name, "Kayla," drips from his tongue like acid.

Nico gives the smallest nod. "She's under his control, too." He looks furtively from Kole to Nova. "She was his mate, but he rejected her when she was pregnant with me. Left her for a human." He glances at Sam. "A woman called Elena."

As the pieces of his past both blur and slide into place at the same time, Sam looks like he might vomit. Nova clasps his hand tight with hers.

"If you came here to tell us Ragnor's the one controlling the League, you're too late. We already knew that." She draws her shoulders back and tips her chin defiantly. "And if you came here for some kind of happy family reunion—"

"That's not why." For the first time, frustration creeps into Nico's voice. Meeting Nova's eyes, inching forward on the couch, he says, "I came here to tell you what Ragnor is planning. I came to tell you he knows where you are."

SAM

Nico's words have barely left his mouth before all four guys erupt into a chorus of cussing and yelling. Luther bolts for the door and locks it. Mack sends a sharp shock of air swirling around the room, slamming the shutters closed.

Nico's eyes widen. He struggles against his restraints, as if he wants to put his hands in the air and beg them to calm down.

"Let him speak." I stand and turn around so I'm facing them. "I'm not sticking up for him," I tell them. "I just think we should let him speak."

Waving at the guys to shush, Nova nods in agreement. When she turns back to Nico, she says calmly, "Ragnor knows where I am?"

"Yes, he knows. He's known the entire time."

"Then why hasn't he come for me?" Nova's eyes flash with heat.

"Because he's not the one who wants you." Nico's shoulders drop, and he releases a deep sigh. Turning to me, he says, "This isn't going to be easy to hear, Sam."

I don't allow my expression to change; I'm good at that.

"Your mother… she died when you were born."

I grit my teeth.

"Well…" Nico swallows hard, like the words are stuck in his throat. "Ragnor's trying to bring her back." He visibly shudders, but I can't understand what he's saying. "That's what this whole thing has been about. All of it. From the beginning. He joined the League because when Elena died, he was furious with her. Furious she was too weak to survive." Nico shifts in his seat. "He worked his way up the ranks, then made some kind of pact."

"Pact?" Mack breaks Nico's flow.

Nico's face has paled. He raises his bound hands and brushes his hair from his face. "The Phoenix's identity for Elena's life." He moves his gaze to Nova's face. "He promised he'd find the witch the prophecy speaks of—the one destined to stop the underworld rising."

Quietly, Nova says, "In exchange for—"

"In exchange for Elena. When he hands over your name, he'll get Elena back. She'll be…" Nico looks at me. His eyes are apologetic, dark, searching. "She'll be resurrected."

I hear the words coming out of Nico's mouth, but it's like they don't have any meaning. My mind is numb. I *know* he's talking about my mother being brought back from the dead, but I can't make myself feel the impact of it. I have no memories of her. I've never even seen a photograph. I don't know her smile, or her hair, or her scent. But I've dreamed of her. Alone in my cell, for years, I've dreamed of the life we might have had if she'd survived.

As if I'm very high up, looking down on what's happening, I hear Mack ask, "Who did he make the pact with Nico?"

Nico shakes his head and stares down into his lap. When he looks up, there are tears in his eyes. His voice is barely a whisper. "He made his pact with the Devil."

* * *

I CAN'T BREATHE. The room is suddenly, overwhelmingly, stiflingly hot. Cloying warmth presses down on my chest. I bolt for the door. Luther tries to stop me, but I push past him. When I start rattling the handle, he unlocks it so I can throw it open. On the veranda, I grip the railings so hard I think I might snap them in half.

Tanner finds me. While the others talk in urgent voices inside, he puts his hand on my shoulder. He doesn't ask if I'm alright; I guess he already knows the answer.

After a few long minutes, I feel able to stand up straight. I turn and rest my back on the railings.

This time, Tanner plants both hands on my shoulders and meets my eyes. "Breathe," he says. "Just breathe."

"My mom…" The words come out small and thready. "He wants to bring her back?" A sickening mixture of hope and dread swirls in my stomach.

I'm wiping a confused tear from my face when Nova appears at the door. Seeing her face sends a lightning rod of pain to my chest. To bring my mother back, Nova would have to die.

As if she can feel my turmoil, Nova pulls me close and hugs me. "I'm sorry," she says. "I'm so sorry you had to hear this."

I try to shove whatever the fuck I'm feeling down into the pit of my stomach. I used to be good at it. Being around Nova, though, my emotions swim closer to the surface. "Do you believe him?" I look from Nova to Tanner.

Tanner's nose twitches as if he's considering the question carefully.

Before he can answer, Nova says, "I do." Justifying herself, she adds, "He's terrified. It's written all over his face, and I don't believe he's a good enough actor to fake it. He tricked us before because I didn't *want* to see the truth. This time, I'm searching, but all I see is pain."

Closing his eyes, Tanner sighs a little. "I agree," he says.

"Then we should go back inside and hear him out." I stand up straight, push my shoulders back, and tighten my jaw. "We're wasting time out here."

I'm about to stride back inside when Nova catches hold of my arm. "We can stay out here as long as you need to," she says softly. "Really... as long as you need."

Instead of answering her, I pull her to me and kiss her. My lips graze hers, my hands weave into her hair. I lose myself in her, then I force myself to stop.

Back inside, Nico's restraints have been removed. Luther doesn't look happy about it, but with four huge mages staring him down—plus Nova—I can't image him trying anything.

He stands up when he sees me. "Sam, I'm sorry. I told you it would be hard to hear."

"I don't want to talk about my mother," I snarl, the wolf in me flashing its teeth. "Tell us what Ragnor plans to do to Nova."

"I don't know exactly," Nico says, gratefully accepting a glass of water from Mack. He takes two large gulps before continuing. "My mother told me about the pact. That's it."

"With the Devil?" I raise my eyebrows at him.

Interrupting, in a professor-like tone, Mack says, "The Devil, The Shadow King, The Unnamed... he is called many things."

"He's a demon?" Nova asks.

"King of Demons," is Nico's reply. "Ruler of the Underworld."

"The biggest bad of all the big bads," Tanner adds. "I always thought he was a myth."

Nico shakes his head. "He's not a myth. Ragnor and his

men are up at The Hollow right now." He glances at Mack. "His witch—Eve—she's insane, and crazy powerful. She's getting ready to perform some kind of ritual. Something to do with the energy underneath the mansion. Bad energy."

Kole and Tanner exchange a knowing glance. Nico's version of events tallies precisely with what they saw—and felt—when they went into Phoenix Falls yesterday. But they don't let Nico know this.

"Mother said Eve will open some kind of window, Ragnor will give the King Nova's name, and tell him where to find her. In return, he'll…" Nico swallows forcefully and looks at me. In a whisper, he adds, "He'll bring Elena back."

"And then what?" Nova is standing in front of Nico, arms folded. "The big bad demon kills me so he can set his friends free from hell and take over the world?"

Nico doesn't reply, just meets her gaze, and blinks up at her.

"Oh," she says, as if the true weight of the situation is finally dawning on her. "I see." She sits down heavily on the coffee table.

Kole puts a large, Viking-like hand on her shoulder. His fingertips brush against her tattoo. "We won't let that happen," he growls. "We won't let anything hurt you."

"If you want to stop it," Nico says, "you need to stop Eve. Stop the ritual. Then kill Ragnor."

As silence descends on the others, I finally find my voice. "You're okay with killing your father?"

"*Our* father." Nico stands up. Staring at him is like staring at a distorted version of myself. My eyes travel to his wrist and the birthmark. The same as mine. Exactly. "He's evil, Sam. Pure evil. He's brought nothing but pain into this world. He's made my life hell, and my mother's. He took you away from me. He took my dignity, my life, and he wants to take Nova's, too. So, yeah, I'm okay with killing him."

"Why do you care? About Nova?" I stare at him as I wait for his answer.

Without taking his eyes from mine, barely waiting a beat, Nico replies, "Because she saw me. Despite the lies I told her, she saw me." He taps his chest. "She saw inside, and she made me feel—even if it was just for a few days—like I was worth something." He looks down at his hands. "No one has ever done that for me before."

Nico's words are so raw I almost expect Nova to take his hand and tell him everything will be okay. Of course, she doesn't. Before she has the chance to say anything at all, Luther growls, "Why don't you do it yourself then?" His question makes everyone look around. He's standing by the window, flicking a lighter with his thumb. Staring past the flame at Nico, he repeats, "If you're okay with killing Ragnor, and so fucking desperate for redemption that you'd come here in the middle of the night to warn us what's about to happen, why haven't you done it? Why haven't *you* killed him?"

With a defeated shrug, Nico laughs. Not a happy laugh—a resigned laugh. Laced with sorrow. "Why haven't I killed him?" He gestures to himself with open palms and laughs again. "Because I'm a fucking coward. A *useless* coward. Ragnor would slit my throat before I got the chance to even give him a paper cut. So, I did the only thing I'm good at—I listened, and learned, and passed on the information to you. Because the six of you are the opposite of cowards. The six of you actually stand a chance."

NOVA

"**Y**ou should go." Mack moves toward the door while looking at Nico. "You've said what you came to say. We need time to discuss what we should do."

For a moment, I expect Nico to object, ask to stay, beg not to be thrown out. But he simply stands up and walks over to Mack. "You have five days," Nico says. "When the moon is full, Eve will perform the ritual."

"Five days." Mack nods at him.

Standing in the doorway, Nico pauses. Without turning to look at me, his shoulders moving heavily up and down as he breathes, he says, "Nova, I truly am sorry for what I did to you. And Sam? I'm sorry we didn't get the chance to know each other."

He's gone before I can reply.

"I'll make sure he leaves." Luther slips out the door, and I hear his heavy footsteps follow Nico down the steps.

As if I'm breathing for the first time in almost an hour, I lean forward with my hands on my knees and suck in a deep gasp of air. Mack's hand on my side makes me stand up straight. Smiling a little, he brushes his finger across the top of my dress. "Why don't you change, Little Star? I'll make tea. Then we'll talk."

I don't want to talk. I want to curl into his arms and disappear. I want him to kiss me until I forget everything I've just heard. I don't want to discuss how we stop a maniac from raising the dead, or an unbeatable demon from slaughtering me in my sleep. I don't want to talk about prophecies or the end of the world.

I just want to lie down with the men who love me and forget that anything else exists.

"Come with me?" I ask him, searching his face. "Please."

Mack looks at the others.

"It's all right, Baloo. You take care of her. We can manage the tea." Tanner cocks his head in the direction of the kettle then says, "Right, Sam?"

"Right," Sam agrees, although he looks like he could use some taking care of, too.

Wrapping his arm around me, Mack guides me to the bathroom. He flicks on the shower, then stands in front of me. Gently, he peels off my dress. When I'm naked, steam swirling around me, he strips out of his tuxedo, picks me up —as if I weigh no more than a bag of feathers—and carries me into the shower. Lowering me to my feet, he smooths his hands over my body. I wrap my arms around him and press my face to his chest so I can hear his heart beating.

For a long time, we just stand under the water. He holds me, without speaking or moving. Just holds me. When we finally step out, he wraps a towel around me and kisses my forehead.

"Wait there. I'll fetch you some clothes." Slinging a towel around his waist, he darts from the room. When he returns, he's holding a large white shirt. "I think this is Luther's?" he says. "The clothes are a mess up there."

His tone of voice makes me smile a little. "Us pesky kids should tidy up after ourselves, huh?"

Mack raises his eyebrows at me. "Wouldn't hurt," he replies, handing over the shirt and watching me button it up.

"Looks good on you," he says, kissing my still-damp forehead.

Sitting down on the closed toilet lid, I brace my hands on my knees. "Is Sam okay?"

"He's talking to Tanner and Kole."

"Is he *okay?*" I repeat the question.

"I think so." Mack's answer is diplomatic but doesn't make me feel any better.

"After what Nico told him, his head must be an utter mess. Ragnor wants to bring his mother back. His *mother.*"

"Tanner and Kole are taking care of Sam. What about you?" Mack crouches on the floor. He's swapped his towel for gray sweatpants. The kind that hang deliciously from his sculpted hips. "So far, you've taken all this in your stride, Nova. You've been through so much and you've just gotten stronger and stronger. But we're talking about your *life* now. We're talking about—"

"I know." I snap at him, then shake my head at myself and soften my tone. "I know, but what choice do I have? I'm part of this. I have no idea why, or how I'm supposed to suddenly become powerful enough to stop what's going to happen, but I do believe I'm part of it. So, I guess I just have to trust that when the time comes, I'll know what to do."

Mack studies my face. Lacing his fingers together at the back of my head, he kisses me. Where once he was unsure, now he is passion personified. He leaves me breathless, my heart beating fast. "We'll figure it out," he says. "We'll figure out a plan."

* * *

"So?" Luther asks loudly, drinking whiskey even though the rest of us are drinking tea and we thought we'd gotten rid of the last of his supply. "What's the plan?"

A resounding silence greets his question until Kole speaks up and says, "The plan hasn't changed. We speak to my mother. Gather as much information as we can about the prophecy, and why Nova's a part of it. Then we return here in time to stop the ritual."

"Why not skip the homecoming visit and go straight to destroying Eve and Ragnor?" Luther replies darkly.

"Because we barely escaped with our lives when they had us in their clutches before," Kole snarls. "So, we'll need more than just a few spells and some good luck."

"And you think your mom will be able to help us? Give us more than just a few spells?" Luther's voice is steady, but the question makes Kole scowl at him.

"I think it's a better idea than charging up to The Hollow with no idea how we'll even get past the forcefield they've got up."

Stepping in, aware of the heat building between his friends, Tanner calmly says, "Luther, Kole's right. You weren't there, you didn't feel the darkness. The energy surrounding the place, it's like nothing I've ever felt before." He glances at me. "And, yeah, Nova's more powerful than she was. But she's not *defeat The Shadow King* powerful."

"Not yet." I'm surprised to hear my own voice. Looking around at each of them in turn, I try to inject confidence into my voice. "I'm not that powerful yet, but maybe if we know more about the prophecy itself, we'll figure out how I can be."

"In that case." Kole turns his back to Luther. "We should get packing. We have a train to catch."

KOLE

"I've never travelled by train before." Nova is hanging onto the open carriage wall, air pummeling her face as she stares out at the fast-moving night.

"Me neither." Sam is next to her. The two of them share something. An innocence. A sense of wonder at the world around them because they spent so much of their young lives living in pain. It's the same lightness that quivers in Tanner sometimes. The lightness Nova does a good job of bringing back, but which can't ever stay thanks to what the League made him do for them.

"Not the most salubrious for your first train journey." Mack brushes his lips across Nova's forehead. Something has changed between the two of them at the ball. It's almost as if I can see a heaviness has lifted, just a little, from his shoulders and he seems more at ease with her now. More at peace. It's good to see him like this.

Luther, on the other hand, is still in a dark place. Hunched in the corner of the carriage, alone, he is pretending to sleep so he doesn't have to interact with us. Seeing how much this is eating him up, I've softened toward the idea of him and Nova being together. But he has to make the first move—he has to tell her how he feels, or at least take a step toward telling her. If he allows himself to wallow in his own misery much longer, I really will be pissed.

Sitting down next to Tanner, he and I watch as Mack shows Nova and Sam a map of our route up toward the Fore Valley. "I didn't know you'd been going home," he says quietly—not looking at me.

I twist my beard between my thumb and forefinger. "No one knew."

"Right." He rubs his knees, then goes to join the others.

Seeing me alone, Nova leaves Sam and Tanner with Mack and comes to sit next to me. Her warmth makes me sigh. She tucks herself under my arm and rests her head on my chest.

You okay? Her voice rumbles through me.

I'm okay. I stroke her hair from her neck. It's still a little curly from her outing with Mack, and smells of whatever stuff Rev sprayed in it. I prefer when she smells like herself. No creams or lotions. I stroke the spot on her neck that still bears the shadow of my teeth marks. Her mouth opens and a small whimper escapes.

Why do I keep thinking about it? she asks silently, curling her fingers around mine. *The way it felt when you...*

I clear my throat and sit up a little straighter. I can't talk to her about this. Not here. Not now. I won't be able to control myself if I think she wants it as badly as I do. Changing the subject, I say out loud, "Tanner's not happy with me."

A flicker of disappointment crosses Nova's face, but then she gives in and follows my line of conversation instead of her silent one. "Why?"

I grind my teeth as I try to find the right words. "Because I didn't tell him I'd been going home."

"You didn't tell Mack or Luther either," she says.

"No, I didn't."

"But you and Tanner would usually share something like that?" She's not jealous, just curious, watching my face carefully.

"Usually."

"So, why didn't you tell him?"

I look down at her. Navigating the relationship that the four—or five—of us now share with her is difficult. I want to explain, but it's not my place to reveal Tanner's truth. He needs to be the one to do that when and if he's ready.

Picking my words carefully, I say, "Because his family couldn't forgive him for his past. It didn't feel right to tell him that mine could." I stop; she still doesn't know how Tanner came into our lives all those years ago or the things he did when he was under the League's control.

"He's an empath, understanding other peoples' feelings is what he does." Nova smiles at me. "He'll soften up." Then she nudges my ribs. "If he doesn't, I'm sure you could find a way to persuade him to."

A low rumble fills my chest. It's been too long since I held her. Too long since I was inside her, and now we have a full night's journey ahead of us. Stuck in this moving carriage with nothing else to do.

It seems Nova's thinking the same as me because she says, "You missed some fun the other day," cocking an eyebrow as she looks over at Sam. "Why didn't you join us?"

Behind closed lips, I run my tongue over my teeth. *I'm not sure I can hold back.* I touch her neck again. She closes her eyes and leans into my fingers.

What if I don't want you to?

It's not a good idea, Nova. Your blood does something to me. It doesn't make me crazy like it should. It makes me stronger. It makes my powers stronger.

So, then—

But that doesn't mean it will always be that way. We've been lucky so far but if something changes, I could hurt you. I look down at her, so small and perfect it makes my heart ache. "I've done a lot of bad things in my life, Nova." I stroke her face. "But I couldn't live with myself if that happened."

"The others are here." She looks over at Mack, Tanner, and Sam. "They won't let you hurt me."

For a moment, my resolve holds. But as my blood pumps louder in my ears, and the sound of her heartbeat fills my soul, I can't stop myself from kissing her. With the heat between us rising, I fuck her mouth with my tongue. I show her all the things I'd like to be doing to her right now, and she welcomes it. She goes limp in my arms, lets me fold myself over her and crowd her with my body.

She's wearing jeans, knee-high boots, and my big black hoodie. I snake my hands up underneath it, desperate to feel her soft skin beneath my rough hands.

Kneeling, I lift her onto the large wooden crate behind us and smooth my hands down her legs. She grins at me then bites her lower lip. By the stars, she's so fucking sexy right now I can barely control myself.

I feel Tanner before I see him. He's drawn to her like a magnet; there's no way he could just stand by and watch while I strip our girl. Bending next to me, he unzips one boot while I take the other. Moving together we work our way farther up to tug off her jeans.

"This too." Sam's voice makes me look up. He's pointing to the hoodie, the arousal in his pants obvious.

When Nova peels my top over her head, she shivers. The open carriage is freezing and, for a moment, I wonder whether it's a good idea to get my dick out. But then she waves her hands and, just like that, the air gets warmer. Usually, she'd use flames but this time she's warming it without fire. With just her mind?

I exchange a look with Mack. He seems both proud and intrigued at the same time. Moving closer, he stands beside her and tips her face up toward him. Before he kisses her, he says, "How did you do that, Little Star?"

Nova meets his gaze, then smiles at him. "Magick, Professor." She scratches his chin playfully. "Magick." Then she gives her legs a little kick and stands up. Putting her hands behind her back, standing in front of us in just black panties and her turquoise bra, she says, "As we've got a few hours to kill, I'd like to play a game."

The four of us wait for her to continue, each captivated by her brightness.

"I have four boyfriends," she says, a smile stretching her lips as she shakes her head. "I didn't think I'd find one guy who treats me the way you four do, or who makes me *feel* the way you do." As she emphasizes the word 'feel', she smooths her hands over her stomach and sighs. "But I'm wondering just how far you'll go to make me happy?"

Nova raises her eyebrows at us. The confidence that flutters in the air around her makes my dick pulse in my pants. Fuck, she's beautiful. And she's starting to believe it.

"What do you want us to do, Little Star?" Tanner asks eagerly, brushing his hair from his face and exchanging an excited grin with Sam.

"You don't have to do much, actually," she says. "Just take your clothes off and stand in a line."

"Take our clothes off?" Mack asks, never afraid to strip off. "And stand in a line?"

Nova nods. She sidles over to Mack and drags her index finger down his chest, pausing when she gets to his pants. "Well done, Professor, you're paying attention."

"Then what?" Mack asks stoically.

"Then you're going to blindfold me, and we're going to play a guessing game." She looks purposefully down at

Mack's crotch. "We're going to see if I can recognize you—*all* of you—using nothing but my mouth."

Mack swallows hard as Nova runs her tongue over her lower lip.

"But you're not allowed to say a word, and you're not allowed to move." She looks at us each in turn. "Got it?"

All a little speechless, we nod at her. Barely a second later, we start to strip.

When our clothes are in bundles on the floor, Nova walks to her backpack and starts rummaging around in it. Bent over, ass in the air, none of us can look away.

"Holy hell," Sam mutters, his scarred but toned body illuminated by the moonlight trickling in from outside. "Is she really going to…?" He looks at Tanner, who grins at him.

When Nova returns, she's holding a silk scarf. "Rev told me to wear it to keep the curls in," she says, holding it up. "Who wants to tie it?"

Mack steps forward—of course, he does. Gently, he folds it in half then wraps it around her face. He ties it tight at the back of her head, then adjusts it so it's flush against her closed eyes. "Can you see me?"

Nova shakes her head. "Not a thing." She's about to say something else when Tanner interrupts.

"Don't you think…" he says, reaching back into Nova's bag, "we should help you resist the temptation to use your hands?"

A shiver shakes Nova's arms. She doesn't reply, just stands still, and puts her hands behind her back.

Silently, Tanner uses one of Nova's tank tops to bind her wrists, twisting it and fixing it tight so she can't break free. He kisses her forehead when he's done.

"Okay," she says, her breasts jutting out as she wriggles a little, testing Tanner's knot. "Time to line up, boys."

Like a bunch of hormonal teenagers with raging erections, we position ourselves in front of her, moving around a couple of times so she has no idea who is where.

Behind us, Luther mutters, "Seriously? This is how we're spending our time? Shouldn't we be—"

Mack is the one who cuts him off. "Shut the fuck up, Luther," he growls.

"Yeah, Luther," Tanner adds, "if you don't want to join in the fun, that's fine. But don't ruin the party for the rest of us."

At that, Luther is silent. But then we have to rearrange ourselves again because Nova heard exactly where Mack and Tanner's voices came from.

"Okay," she says, "I'm ready." She's about to walk forward when she says, "Luther? Could you point me in the right direction? Bit worried I'll fall out of the train if I misjudge."

There's a moment of quivering silence, then Luther stands up and stomps toward her. When he positions himself behind her and takes her roughly by the waist, a growl rumbles in my chest. Without an ounce of softness, he marches her forward and stands her in front of Sam. "There," he says gruffly. "Get on your knees and you'll find what you're looking for."

As she drops to the ground, Luther lingers behind her. I watch his eyes. They are dark and brimming with something I can't put a name to. When he screws them shut and strides back to his corner, I *almost* feel sorry for him.

On the floor in front of Sam, Nova inches forward until her knees touch his feet. She puts her tongue to his inner thigh and traces a long line up toward his balls. When she reaches them, instead of taking them in her mouth, she keeps going. She laps at the groove of his hips, the spot where a small line of hair creeps down from his belly button. His dick nudges her cheek, but she ignores it.

Sam grasps his hair and bites his lip, desperately trying not to make a sound.

Finally, Nova makes contact with his shaft. She runs her lips up the side, then sweeps her tongue over the tip. When she takes him in her mouth, she pushes the head against the inside of her cheek then changes position and takes him as far down her throat as she can.

Sam looks like he's ready to explode. His face is flushed, and a line of sweat has broken out on his torso. He reaches out as if he's about to take hold of her head and thrust deeper into her mouth, but then stops himself.

Seconds later, she has left him wet and exposed, and she's moving on to Mack.

NOVA

Kole is last in the line. Even if I hadn't already guessed the others, I'd have known it was him because the second my lips touch his skin my heart nearly beats right out of my chest.

A hot, rushing sensation floods my veins. My neck begins to pulse and then, as I position myself beneath him and take his balls in my mouth, a silent groan of pleasure fills my head.

You gave yourself away, I tell him without speaking.

I can't control myself around you, he replies.

Taking my lips away from him, I sit back and enjoy the way the air quivers with heat. The four of them are so primed, and so ready. I've worked them into a stupor and now I'm going to let them have me.

The thought of how much they desire me right now is so fucking liberating, it's almost enough to make me draw it out longer. But I can't do that because I'm in a stupor, too.

"Sam, Mack, Tanner, Kole," I say confidently. As they ask, "How did you know?" and, "What gave me away?" I laugh and wriggle against my restraints. "Because I've memorized your taste," I tell them. "Now, let me loose, so I can show how grateful I am to you for being such good sports."

I turn my wrists toward them and wait, but no hand comes. No one undoes the knot. No one removes the blindfold.

I feel them moving toward me. Their energy crowds me and makes me suck in a deep, sudden breath. A cluster of tiny fireworks heads for my core, and suddenly everything is heightened. In the dark, the sound of the train on the tracks, the vibration as it moves, the rush of air outside the carriage all feels louder, and stronger, and more powerful.

My skin is alive, too. It reminds me of the way I felt the night I arrived in Phoenix Falls—like there are a million more nerve endings than there were before, and each of them is being lit up.

A pair of heavy hands takes my arms and pull me to my feet. Before I've had chance to decide whose hands they were, someone is kissing me. It's Tanner; I'd know his lips anywhere. I lose myself in him, my tongue welcoming his urgently into my mouth.

My bra is unclasped. It's peeled off my shoulders with achingly slow fingers, then hangs half-obscuring my breasts while another pair of hands peels my black underwear down over my hips.

My legs are parted, causing me to wobble a little, but someone is behind me keeping me steady. A tongue works in small delicate circles up my inner thigh, then another kisses the backs of my knees—a spot I'd never have even dreamed would be erotic until I met my mages.

Even though I know there are only four of them, I feel like there are a hundred hands on me. A hundred tongues. Like my body is lighting up in a hundred different places all at once. Pulses of electricity shoot to where their lips and hands meet my skin, creating miniature explosions that make me hum and groan.

A mouth clamps down hard on my nipple. I gasp as my hard bud is sucked and nibbled; pain merging with pleasure and becoming something else. Something bigger.

I am desperate to touch them, to feel their bodies, to explore the cords of muscle that create glorious rivets on their chests. I'm desperate to wrap my fingers around them and enjoy their arousal. But I can't move. My hands are bound.

"Let me touch you," I plead, with no idea who I'm speaking to.

"Not yet, Little Star," Mack whispers in my ear. I turn my head toward his voice and steal his words from his mouth with a hungry kiss. He kisses me back, then hands—not Mack's—are beneath my ass. I'm being scooped up into someone's arms. Tanner. It has to be Tanner because his chest is smooth and he smells of morning rain. I don't know how a person can smell like rain, but he does. My Tanner does.

There's a shuffling sound as Tanner lowers me to the floor, landing me on a blanket. It's not soft, but softer than the bare wooden floor would be. Finally, my wrists are set free. My bra falls to the floor and I reach for the blindfold, but a hand stops me.

"Keep it on," Kole whispers. "Everything is brighter in the dark." As if to prove it, he trails a wet finger down between my breasts, over my stomach, toward my center. When he reaches my clit, he stops. I try to move with him, but his hand has disappeared.

I'm reaching for him when my fingers find Sam's erection instead. Hungrily, I take my lips to his shaft. He weaves his fingers into my hair and pulls my mouth onto him. As I suck and lap and moisten his cock, a tongue starts toying with my clit.

A long, thick finger enters my pussy, then another, and I have no idea if they belong to just one of my boyfriends or two of them. I'm in heaven. Actual heaven. I can't think; all I can do now is feel. Their hands, their lips, the way they want me.

It should be strange, or taboo, or confusing, or dirty. Except, it's not. Being with them like this feels like the most natural thing in the world. As love and lust swirl around us, I finally pull the blindfold from my face.

Tanner and Sam are between my legs, kissing each other while they play with my pussy. The sight makes my eyes roll back in my head and my toes curl viciously. Leaning back, I realize Mack is behind me. He's stroking my hair, running his hands down my body, easing the excruciating arousal that's flooding my body.

"Baby girl," he mutters, "you look so fucking good with two men sucking your clit."

My eyes flash as they meet his. Finally, he's telling me what he likes.

As Mack holds my chin and eases his shaft into my mouth, Kole strokes my stomach, his big firm hands travelling up and down my body like he's trying to memorize every inch of it. Then he stops, nudges Tanner and Sam out of the way and flips me over onto my front. Before I have chance to fully open my legs, Kole plunges into me. He arches over me, pressing me flat to the floor, his weight suffocating and exhilarating at the same time.

My fingers scrunch the blanket hard. It shifts beneath me. Soon, my nails are scratching the wooden floor as I cry out with pleasure.

When Kole leaves me, I feel empty, but only for a moment because then Mack is taking his place, turning me back over so I'm facing him. Taking gentle hold of my ankles, Mack lifts my legs and hooks them over his shoulders. Instantly, my arms fly to my stomach. I can't think of a more unflattering angle, and my bravado starts to melt.

Mack snatches my hands away. As he slides into my cunt, his eyes fix on mine. "Look at me," he growls. "You're ours. Do not disrespect what's ours. Every inch of you is perfect."

A breathless simper escapes my lips. I turn and look for Tanner. He and Sam are watching, giving their dicks long, firm strokes as they study Mack's punishing thrusts. Crawling up the side of my body, Tanner kisses me. I tip my head back, and he understands what I want.

Positioning himself on top of me, so I can take his balls in my mouth and his cock in my hands, he stars to play with my clit. At the exact moment Mack changes angle and finds a spot that makes me yell, Tanner lowers his lips to my pussy. I'm moaning onto his balls when I notice hands on Tanner's ass. Peeking, I see Kole is spreading him open.

Holy hell... I let go of Tanner's dick and stretch my hands back, fire licking my insides as I feel Kole ease his shaft past Tanner's tight ring.

Tanner is still for a moment, then pushes back. Mack tugs me toward him, then angles me so that Tanner can lower his lips to my nipples while Kole fucks him.

Sam is watching them with wide eyes. He's stopped touching himself, as if he's too hypnotized by what he's seeing to move. "Sam," I whisper, "would you like to know what Tanner's dick tastes like?"

"Fuck," Tanner whispers onto my nipple. He looks up with a grin on his face. "Is that what you want, Little Star?"

I nod, barely able to breathe from the crushing heat in my lungs.

As Mack lowers my legs and arches over me, pulling me into a hold so tight I feel like the weight of a polar bear is on top of me instead of a man, Sam gently wraps his lips around Tanner's shaft.

The three of them rock back and forth, and they're so fucking beautiful I can't look away.

"Daddy," I plead, grabbing onto Mack, "I need to come. Please...."

With a growl, Mack quickens his pace and thrusts a hand between my legs. When my orgasm approaches, and my body stiffens, the others sense it. They let each other go and come to me. Tanner and Sam attack my breasts with their tongues, while Kole grips my hands and kisses me.

I turn my head, exposing my neck. I feel him tense. *Nova...*

Please. I need you. Please. I beg him.

I'm so close, but I know the only thing that will drive me over the edge is the feeling of his teeth puncture my skin. Before I can plead with him again, Kole lets out a roar that shakes the cabin and brings his mouth to my throat. Mack reaches out to stop him, but I grab his hand. Heat rushes to my palm. Mack cries out as his skin sizzles. "Don't stop him," I growl. "Don't... stop..."

23

LUTHER

Nova's words are snatched from her mouth by the thunderous orgasm that decimates her body. Fireworks explode on her skin. Sparks dance in the air around her while tears come to her eyes.

The others are all staring at Kole. So fucking lost in how much they want her that they're unwilling to disobey her.

I'm about to stand up and wrench his teeth from her neck when, somehow, he does it himself. He pulls himself away from her. When she looks up and sees her blood trickling down his chin, the orgasm that was fading rushes back. She clenches her fists, locks her legs around Mack's waist, and makes noises I've never heard coming from a woman's mouth before.

As she trembles and collapses into a sweaty heap, the others continue kissing and stroking and soothing her while she rides the crescendo of her orgasm, Nova's eyes latch onto mine.

She keeps my gaze as Mack comes inside her, holding her hands tight while his hot liquid fills her up. Standing to one side, Sam's eyes widen as he and Tanner paint her breasts white. She pulls Sam down and kisses him forcefully, like she's trying to taste Tanner in his mouth.

Apart from me, Kole is the only one who hasn't come. How he's lasted this long, I have no idea. His dick is so hard it looks almost painful. Blood stains his lips.

Nova beckons him to her. "I can't," he growls, wiping his mouth with the back of his hand. His eyes are black and he's clearly fucking terrified that if he bites her a second time, he might not be able to stop himself.

He's kneeling, his large knuckles white with pressure as he holds his throbbing dick.

"Yes, you can." Nova eases herself off Mack's shaft then turns onto all fours and crawls toward him. Kole watches her, entranced. Mack watches too, with a prime view of her ass.

When she reaches Kole's lap, she plunges her mouth onto his shaft and takes it so far back that she gags. Spikes of electricity shoot to my center. I can't take it any longer. I stand and turn around, so I can't see them. Then I shove my hand into my pants and fist myself hard. Fast. Ugly.

When Kole comes, he roars so loudly the whole fucking carriage rattles. Part of me wanted him to stride over and enter me, like he did at the cabin. Fuck some relief into me.

When a hand lands on my shoulder, I spin around, but it's not Kole—it's her.

Completely naked, with blood trickling from her throat, Sam's cum on her chest, and Mack's leaking from her cunt, she puts her hand on me. All the time, never looking away from my eyes. She stares up at me, small and delicate but vibrating with power. Power over the elements. Power over the five of us.

As I watch her grab me and slowly stroke my pierced shaft, anger rolls through me in waves. I'm angry with her. Fucking furious. She makes my blood boil. She brings fire to my veins, and heat to my soul. Except, I can't be furious with her because—mixed in with the anger—is something pure. Something that might be love if I looked at it hard enough.

She licks her lower lip, bites the corner, and tightens her grip on me. "Would it help if I gave you something to bury your face in?" she asks, blinking up at me. "I have some spare underwear in my bag."

She's making fun of me? She's got her hand around my dick and she's mocking me? Without thinking, I grab her shoulders and push her down to the floor.

I feel the others move toward me—a wall of testosterone ready to beat my ass if I hurt her. But she's not hurt; she's opening her legs for me. Picking them up, wrapping them tight around my waist, I plunge into her. She's so wet I'm struggling to gain traction, so I pound harder. She cries out and screws her eyes closed, but I don't want that. I want her to look at me.

Arching one arm over her head, I cup her face with my other hand. When she opens her eyes, I let out a loud groan and slam once, twice, three times deep into her core.

"Luther..." She breathes my name, steals a kiss from my half-open lips, then moans into my mouth as I unload violently inside her—my name on her lips sending me over the edge.

My body shakes. She squeezes every last drop from me, then buries her head in my neck.

As I tremble inside her, she whispers, "Do you still hate me? Or are we making progress?"

I don't reply.

* * *

A WHILE LATER, when the others are sleeping, Nova unfurls herself from the middle of their tight little bundle and pads over to where I'm sleeping. Alone. Propped up against a large wooden crate.

"Luther?" She sits next to me and pulls the blanket so it covers us both.

I don't reply or open my eyes.

"I know you're awake," she whispers.

"No," I say, "I'm not." But when she sighs and moves as if she's about to leave, I give in. "Okay. I'm awake." I look down at her. Her neck is bruised and ugly. Kole's not a vamp, so he makes a hell of a fucking mess when he bites her. "Are you alright?" I touch my fingers to the wound.

Nova doesn't flinch, just leans into me a little. "I wanted it," she says as if that answers my question. Frowning, she picks at a loose thread in the blanket. "Luther?"

"Yes." I can't get enough of the way she says my name. I look away from her because my dick is starting to pay attention to her, and I'm pretty sure she's had enough for one night.

"I can't be the only one to have noticed that there are five of you here," she says.

"Last I counted," I reply.

"And the prophecy says *fated to five*."

"It does." I can feel her staring at me, and I finally give in.

When I meet her eyes, she says, "Is that why I feel the way I do when I'm around you?"

I swallow hard. My heart beats fast in my chest. Clearing my throat, I ask hoarsely, "How exactly do you feel?"

"Like I want to kill you and fuck you at the same time," she laughs. "Like if I let you get too close, I'll get hurt. But like I want you so much I don't care."

As her words sink into my skin, I rub my palm over my shaved head. "You think I'd hurt you?" Does she see the irony? She thinks *I'll* hurt her, but Kole's the one drinking her blood?

After a moment's silence, she replies, "It's not a thought. It's a feeling... like if I let myself fall for you it's destined to end badly."

"You don't feel that way about the others?"

"No," she says. "I don't."

A cross between rejection and anger hums on my skin. At the same time, I feel vindicated. I knew there was a reason I shouldn't let myself fall for this woman. She doesn't trust me. She sees something in me that I've always seen in myself. She knows I'm no good for her. "Then you should trust your gut," I tell her, turning away and jerking the blanket from her lap. "And stay the fuck away from me."

24

TANNER

The screech of metal-on-metal jolts me awake. Kole's head is on my stomach. His hair is loose, with one arm stretched up above his head so his fingers touch the base of my throat. Nova's sleeping on his chest, curled into him like a kitten, and his other arm is wrapped tightly around her. Even in his sleep, he's keeping her close.

Behind Nova, Sam's arms are looped around her waist, his knees tucked up beside hers. He's been through the most out of all of us, yet somehow manages to look so *at peace* when he sleeps. Perhaps it's just because he's finally with Nova. Safe.

When I look up, Mack and Luther are already awake and watching me. Mack's sitting with his back against a large wooden crate. Luther, sitting next to him, slides his bag over so I can position it behind Kole's head and slide out from beneath him.

He stirs, sweeps his lips over Nova's forehead without waking, and moves the arm that was slung over my torso to hug her instead.

"They look so content, don't they?" I ask, pushing my hair back from my face and smiling at them. I don't think I'll ever get bored of seeing Nova like that; cocooned, safe, happy.

"We're nearly there," Luther says. He's avoiding looking at me. He lost control last night. It doesn't sit well with him but if he's expecting me to be pissed, he's wrong. I just wish he'd get the fuck over himself and admit he needs Nova as much as the rest of us.

"Let them sleep," Mack says, although he looks like he hasn't caught more than a few minutes since we boarded the train.

"Is it a long journey to the commune?" I accept the flask of almost-cold coffee Luther's offering and take a long sip. I wince then raise my eyebrows at him. Obliging, slightly reluctantly, he wraps his hands around it and heats it for me.

"I'm not sure." Mack pulls his cell from his pocket and pinches the map to zoom in on the area where we're expecting to find Kole's family. "Maybe an hour? Two?"

I sit back and pay attention to the warmth of the coffee as it slides down my throat. Outside the carriage, scenery rushes past at a speed that makes my ears fizz. "Did you know?" I look from Mack to Luther. "That he'd been visiting?"

They both shake their heads, which makes me feel marginally better; at least it wasn't just me who got left out of the loop.

"Maybe he thought you'd..." Mack trails off. He's not often lost for words but an awkward hesitation hums around him.

"It's okay," I tell him. "You can say it—maybe he thought it would make me sad to know that his family can forgive the things he did whereas mine can't stand to look at me anymore?"

Mack presses his lips together and nods a little.

"That's not the reason—" Kole's voice makes me turn around. He's still hugging Nova, but he's looking at me.

I wait for him to explain.

Gently, Kole sits up. It makes Nova stir and, when she moves, Sam does too. As they yawn and blink at the dim morning light of the carriage, Kole scrapes his hair back to expose the ink on his neck. "At least, not all of the reason." He crosses his arms. "I didn't want anyone to know I'm still in contact with them because I didn't want them to be in danger."

Something flashes in my gut. Hurt and indignation. "You mean you didn't want them to be used against you? Used to manipulate you? The way mine were?" I stand and stride over to him.

Kole rises slowly. He's taller than me and broader than me. Looking at him right now, I have no idea if I want to punch him or fuck him. "Yes," he says, meeting my eyes.

"You didn't trust that we'd keep your secret?" I glance back at Luther and Mack, who are still sitting down, watching as if they have no intention of getting involved.

As we stare at one another, Nova scrambles to her feet. She puts her hand on my arm and tilts her head to meet my eyes, "Tanner? What's going on?"

Sam stands too but moves over beside Mack. He still looks half asleep.

"Tanner?" Nova asks again, smiling a little. "Everything okay?"

I open my mouth to explain, but no words come out. Kole's done nothing wrong. He saw what the League did to my family—what they made me do, using my parents as leverage—and took steps to prevent the same thing happening to him or his own people. It just hurts to know I never got that chance.

I meet Kole's gaze. He puts his hands into his pockets and

just stands there waiting, as if he knows I'm about to realize my anger isn't meant for him. He nods at me. My muscles untense. Kole squeezes my shoulder then gestures to the flask I'm holding. "That for sharing?"

I pass it over.

"Okay?" he asks.

"Okay."

Watching us, Nova frowns. Her face is delightfully crumpled, lines from Kole's t-shirt on her cheek, her hair all kinds of messy after our group activities last night. "What just happened?" she asks, folding her arms in front of her stomach. "What did I miss?"

"I'll explain later," I promise her. "It's nothing to worry about. I was being an asshole."

"No, you weren't," Kole says gruffly. "But you're right, the explanation can wait." He walks over to the open side of the carriage and hangs on to it as he sticks his head out. Pointing into the distance, at the shadowy silhouette of a mountain range and the swathes of forest in front of it, he says, "Almost our stop. Hope you've all got your crash helmets ready."

* * *

"I THOUGHT we were heading for a train station?" Nova puts her hands on her hips. "You're telling me we've got to leap from a moving train? That sounds ridiculously unsafe."

"It'll slow down as it passes through the next station, but it's a cargo train. No stops." Kole picks up his backpack and shrugs it onto his shoulders, then turns to the crates behind us. With one swift blow, barely stopping for breath, he smashes one open. Small plastic beads spill out onto the floor of the train along with at least two-hundred yellow rubber ducks.

"Help me with this," Kole turns to me as he breaks the lid off.

I take it from him as he pulls the rest of the crate apart, then turns to another and does the same. When he's finished, we're standing in a field of yellow ducks and plastic beads looking at a stack of wooden crate pieces.

"Couldn't have been crates of booze, could it?" Luther mutters.

"We jump at the same time. Just past the station there's a section of track with a slope on this side. It goes down into the forest." Kole hands Mack one of the crate pieces then gestures for everyone else to take one. "Start at the back." He jerks his head over his shoulder. "Running jump." He pats the piece of wood he's holding. "Land on this like it's a sled, belly down, and slide down the slope into the trees." He looks around the group. "Okay?"

As the rest of us nod, Nova's face pales. I tell her, "You'll be fine. The running jump counteracts the train's velocity. The sled softens the impact because it helps you keep moving fast."

She frowns at me.

"Science nerd," I reply, shrugging and smiling reassuringly at her. "Trust the science."

"Right." Nova hugs her new wooden sled to her chest. "Trust the science."

A few minutes later, we're lined up at the back of the carriage, ducks and beads kicked out of the way, ready to hurtle to our death. Kole is hanging out of the carriage watching for the station. "Here it is." He runs back to us and positions himself next to Nova.

"Pretend it's that fairground ride," Sam says, nodding at her. "The one that made your dad throw up. Remember?"

A laugh tickles her chest. "Sure. I remember."

"Ready!" Kole yells. "On three..." He starts to count. We grip our sleds tightly. When he reaches three, we run.

25

NOVA

As my feet leave the edge of the train carriage, my heart leaps up into my throat. I'm hurtling toward death—that much is obvious. There's no way Kole's sled trick will work. The wood will shatter. I'll hit the ground stomach-first, so hard my internal organs will get squished up into all the wrong places, and I'll die before I've even had chance to *think* about saving the world.

As I throw myself forward, slamming my belly onto the piece of crate I'm supposed to be using to slide down the hill, I screw my eyes shut and wait for the impact. Something is underneath me, but it's not solid ground. I open one eye and look sideways to see Mack throwing a current of air in my direction.

So instead of hitting the ground with a huge thump, I swoop down and slide effortlessly into the dense thicket of trees in front of me. As my makeshift sled catches on a tree root, spins sideways, and throws me into the bushes, I hear the others yelling. Mack hurtles past and slams into a tree. Tanner groans, but I can't see where he's landed. As I stand, shakily, Sam's head appears from a bush nearby. A twig is sticking out of it, and he looks comically dizzy. Kole, however, simply skids to a halt and stands as if he's some kind of stunt double in a cheesy action movie.

"Okay, Little Star?" He strides over and puts both hands on my upper arms, examining me closely.

"Fine. Good. Mack gave me a helping hand." I look in Mack's direction. He's rubbing his shoulder.

"Think it's dislocated," he mutters, wincing. "Where's Tanner?"

"I'm here." Tanner's voice drifts through the crevices between the trees. "Hold on." When he emerges, he looks in a better state than Mack or Sam. Not quite as suave as Kole though. "Ouch," he says, wincing as he looks at Mack's shoulder. "Sorry, Baloo, you're right. Dislocation."

Mack growls. He's pale and sweat has broken out on his forehead. "Can you pop it back in?" he asks.

Tanner grimaces. "It'll hurt like fuck, but yeah I can put it back in." He cocks his head toward the shadows. "Come over here. We don't need an audience."

I move to go with them, but Tanner shakes his head. "It's not nice to watch, Little Star. Stay here. Baloo will be fine."

When they've disappeared, so I don't have to wait for the sound of Mack's shoulder being yanked back into place, I turn and scan the trees for Luther. Kole's doing the same.

"He was behind you, right?" I ask, my heart catching in my chest. "We didn't leave him behind, did we? I mean, he wasn't still on the train, was he?" A slow heat creeps up my neck.

"He was next to me," Sam says. "He definitely jumped."

"Wait here," Kole tells me. "We'll go look." He gestures for Sam to follow him. Folding my arms, I tap my foot impatiently. I wait a few more seconds before heading in the other direction.

I'm searching the ground when I notice a white sneaker

sticking out of a bush at a funny angle. I crouch down and move the branches aside. "Luther?" I move up his body then put my hands on his shoulders. His eyes are closed. He's bleeding from a cut on his forehead. "Luther?" I shake him, just a little. He groans and his eyelids flutter, but he doesn't open them.

"It's okay." I move behind him and pull his head into my lap. The strength of the worry that's twisting my insides takes me by surprise. Especially after what he said to me last night.

Raising my voice, I shout for Tanner. The sound makes Luther try to sit up, but I tell him not to move. "Wait. Tanner's coming."

He opens his eyes. Upside down, he looks at me. His eyes travel my face, skimming over my features. They leave a trail of warmth that makes my cheeks flush. "You," he says. "You're so beautiful."

My mouth drops open. Quite literally *drops* open. Last night he told me to stay the hell away from him and now he's telling me I'm beautiful? Not that he wants to fuck me—that I'm *beautiful.*

Before I can reply, his eyes close again and footsteps crunch behind us.

"Nova? I thought you were waiting?" Kole helps me to my feet as Tanner kneels next to Luther.

"Looks like he's hit his head pretty hard." Tanner reaches for his pack and pulls out a medical kit. "I'll clean it up, but he'll need to rest a while. We better set up camp."

No time. We don't have time. Kole's voice sends a shiver through me.

Tanner can't hear him, but he must feel the urgency vibrating on Kole's skin because he looks up and says, "We'll move quicker if we wait for him to wake up. The alternative is to make a stretcher and carry him." Tanner glances at

Luther's bulky frame. "And I'm not sure I'm up for that. Are you?"

For a moment, Kole looks like he might be seriously considering this as an option, but then he shakes his head and stalks back off into the undergrowth.

I'm about to go after him when I glance at Luther. I'm reluctant to leave him. My head knows he'll be fine, but my body is telling me to stay.

"I'll talk to Kole." Sam nods at me as if he can read the dilemma on my face. "I'll tell Mack to come this way. Find some wood to use as kindling." Before he leaves, he brushes his lips across mine. The softness of his kiss, and the way it sends sparks of electricity pulsing through my skin, still takes me by surprise. I squeeze his hand. "Tell Kole we'll get moving as soon as we can."

But, despite Tanner's best efforts, Luther remains unconscious until just before nightfall. When he opens his eyes, he finds me first and tries to sit up.

"It's okay. You banged your head. We're camping here tonight." I look around at the others. Luther follows my gaze. He lifts a hand to his head. "Tanner stitched you up, but you'll have a mean looking scar if you're lucky."

Again, Luther tries to sit up. Kole helps him, and he leans back against the fallen tree trunk we've been using as a wind break.

"What happened to you?" Luther croaks, taking in Mack's makeshift sling.

"Dislocated shoulder."

Again, Luther touches the wound on his head.

"So much for science, huh?" I tease quietly, handing him a bottle of water.

"Never was a particularly good nerd," Luther replies, taking the water and downing three huge gulps that make his throat throb. "Where are we?" he asks when he's finished.

Kole pulls a map from his pack. Out here, our cells are all but useless. "Here." Kole jabs his thick index finger at the map. "Commune's here." He points further north. "A four-hour trek."

"We'll leave at first light." Mack pats Luther's shoulder. "Get some rest."

For a moment, Luther looks like he's going to object, but then he closes his eyes again and is gone.

* * *

BY THE TIME the sun sets, the temperature is dropping, an ominous mist is creeping through the trees and, even with the fire and my jacket, I'm starting to shiver.

Mack is sitting behind me. He rubs my arms then says, "I have a better way to keep you warm." Standing up, looking at Tanner, he says, "Help me take these off."

Tanner frowns.

Mack tugs one arm free from his hoodie but the other is in the sling. "Tanner? Help me with this?" His tone sends a shiver through me. A different kind of shiver this time.

"Yes, Sir," Tanner smiles.

Without asking why, Tanner helps Mack undress. When his clothes are gone— all of them—Mack stands in front of me and shakes his arms. He winces as he moves his injured shoulder.

I raise my eyebrows. Even in the cold, his length is impressive. But I'm not sure I can stand the thought of getting naked with him in weather like this, even if he does look good enough to eat.

With another shake, Mack's jaw twitches. His head moves from side to side. Now I get it; he's going to shift.

The others get it, too. At the same time, we stand and move back to give Mack some room. His muscles bulge, his shoulders grow larger, his limbs crack and jerk as they change. I glance at Sam. He's watching Mack closely.

"I've never seen a bear shift before," he whispers.

As Mack's shoulder jerks up and takes on a new shape, he roars. It's not a human roar. It's a growl. Loud enough to make my core hum with the ferocity of it.

Finally, Mack's gone, and Snow is in his place. The big white bear huffs loudly. A cloud of warm air blooms from his nostrils. He fixes his dark eyes on me, makes a noise I can't quite interpret, then sits down hard on the floor. Growling again—more of a yawn this time—he rolls onto his side and looks up at me.

For a moment, I hesitate but then I understand what he wants. "You want me to come for a cuddle?"

Snow huffs again.

I kneel down and crawl toward him. Even though I know he's Mack, being this close to something so huge and powerful feels unnatural.

I put my hand on his stomach. His fur is thick and soft. As I lie down, Snow curls around me. His limbs are enormous. He could crush me—or eat me—in a second. But all he wants to do is keep me warm. As I let him envelop me, Tanner crouches down and leans onto Snow's hind leg. Sam tucks in next to me. Kole, however, stays with Luther.

"I'll watch him. You four sleep." He looks at Tanner. "We'll switch in a few hours."

Fighting a yawn, Tanner nods. I snuggle down, tucking myself into the warmth of Snow's huge body before finding Sam's hand and squeezing it.

I'm almost asleep when he whispers, "Nova? Do you think Nico's alright? Did we do the right thing? Making him go back to Ragnor?"

I don't open my eyes, just breathe in slowly and whisper back, "I hope so, Sam. I really hope so."

26

KOLE

At first light, we leave the campsite. My body aches with tiredness. Although Tanner offered to swap places with me, in the end I stayed awake all night. Watching. Waiting.

I last saw my mother ten months ago. It is always the same journey. A train, a jump into the trees, then a trek down into the valley. Before going undercover with the League, I visited like any normal son would visit—by road. But after I left, and especially when I found out what the League did to Tanner's family, I vowed I would never put my own people in danger like that.

The commune is protected by old magick. It is unfindable unless you know what you're looking for. So, I did everything I could to keep it that way.

As we move through the forest, Nova hovers next to me. She keeps looking at Luther, but he won't turn his head in her direction. *Something happened between you?* I ask her, sending the question silently through the air between us.

You saw, she replies, arching her eyebrow at me. *You watched.*

Not the sex. After. I meet her gaze. My eyes are dark. I can feel the blackness in them. As we weave through the trees, the energy of the earth pounds in my ribs. Power pulses in my veins. If I wanted to, I could rip up the entire forest and I know it's because I've got Nova's blood inside me. Having her close makes it worse but having her further away would make it worse, too. I shouldn't have bitten her again but how the fuck was I supposed to resist when she was begging me to do it?

I tried to talk to him. It didn't go well. She shrugs and attempts a smile.

I want to put my arm around her. I want to show her the tenderness I feel able to show when we're alone in the dark but, with the others present, it's hard. Something inside me resists.

I don't like that Luther is causing her to feel hurt and confused. I don't like that he fucked her and now he's barely even looking at her. I know *why* he's being this way—because he doesn't let anyone get close, period—but I'm not okay with him doing it to Nova.

If we were back at the cabin, I'd sit him down and tell him to sort himself the fuck out. To stop messing with our girl. But we're not, and there isn't time for that right now.

We're approaching the part of the valley where the ground slopes steeply downward when I start to feel cold. Too cold. The hair on my arms prickles. I'm about to turn around and tell the others to stop when something hits me. Like a brick wall. A blinding light floods my vision. I stumble back, and then the light becomes darkness.

I hear Nova's voice, but it's very far away.

When I look up, it's like I'm at the bottom of a well staring at a pinprick of light. I focus on it, but it grows smaller and smaller until it disappears. A heavy blackness envelops me, stinging my skin like a poisonous mist. I look down at my hands and arms but can barely see them. They're translucent. Not really there at all.

My heart beats faster, thudding in my ears. Fear grips my chest; the same feeling that turned my blood to ice when Tanner and I stood in the trees outside the Hollow.

Everything in my body tells me to run, but I can't.

When I look up, the black mist starts to clear. Heat crawls up my legs. I turn my gaze down to my feet. Red hot vines snake around my calves, thighs, and waist. They burn. I pull against them, reach down, and snap them. My legs are free but when the vines fall, they take strips of my clothes and my flesh with them.

I scream, but no sound comes out.

With open wounds sending torrents of pain through my body, overwhelming my thoughts, I stagger forward. Then I see him. Eyes as black as coal, gray skin stretched tight over an enormous seven-foot frame. Long, gnarled fingernails reach for me. One of them points at my throat. The dagger-like nail pricks my skin, a bead of deep red blood glistening on its tip. He draws the blood to his gaping mouth. When he sucks my blood from his finger, I scream again. I fall to the floor. Pain swallows me up. I am imploding and exploding. His eyes bore into my soul. They take everything. My name, my past, my life. I am nothing but pain.

"Kole? Kole, can you hear me?" A voice breaks through the torment.

I feel something. The whisper of a touch. I latch onto it and try to bring myself back.

"Kole, listen to my voice. Follow my voice. Come back to us." I know that voice. It feels like home.

When I open my eyes, my mother is staring at me.

NOVA

Tanner and Sam practically carry Kole through the trees. His eyes are vacant, swimming with darkness. "The noise he made…" I jog up to Tanner and try to meet his eyes. "The way he screamed," I whisper urgently. My heart is thundering. Hot nausea swells in my stomach.

"He'll be okay." Tanner doesn't sound even a little bit convinced; he looks as scared as I am and he's staring at Kole.

Turning to Mack, I hope to see something more positive in his face, but he's deep in conversation with Luther and—if anything—seems more disturbed than the rest of us.

Kole's mother leads the way down through the valley. Even if she hadn't told us who she was, I'd have known. She is tall like Kole. A cross between an Amazon and a Viking with thick black hair wound into tight brands and piled on top of her head. She wears a long beige robe, a woolen shawl, and bare feet.

Despite her naked soles, she seems not to even feel the coarse ground beneath them and glides effortlessly down the sloped earth.

"What was that?" Sam asks.

"I have no idea." I look at Tanner. "A vision?"

"I think so." Tanner chews the inside of his cheek. "But I haven't seen anything like that before. Ever."

Up ahead, Thessaly pushes some branches aside and beckons for us to follow. We emerge in a large clearing. A circle of tall, pointed tents surrounds a billowing fire pit, but there isn't a soul in sight.

"Here..." Thessaly's voice is like honey and chocolate. Smooth, dark, sweet. "Bring him in here." She pulls aside the opening of the nearest tent and ushers us into its warmth.

Mack and Luther lower Kole onto a pile of pillows. He sits, unmoving, as if he has no idea where he is.

Without speaking, his mother opens a large wooden trunk and pulls out several hessian pouches. There is a small fire in the middle of the tent, smoke escaping through a hole at the top. Atop the fire a black kettle slowly starts to hum. As it boils, she pours hot water into a mug the opens each of the pouches in turn and sprinkles in what looks like different kinds of leaves.

We watch in silence. When she's finished mixing her concoction, she presses the mug into Kole's hands then sits in front of him. Crossing her legs, she reaches out and gently arranges his into the same position. Helping him raise the cup to his mouth, she says, "Drink now, my love."

Kole... I try to reach him, but my words bounce back. The loneliness makes my chest swell with tears.

Glancing over at Luther, for perhaps the first time, I see unadulterated worry etched in his features. He stares at Kole as he drinks, swiping his palm over his closely shaved hair. I look at the stitched-up wound on his head, the shape of his jaw, the compassion in his eyes. Why can't he show me that same compassion? Why does he look at me with frustration and anger instead of warmth? Even when we were fucking, he hated that he wanted me. I could feel it.

"Mom?" Kole's voice is like gravel. He's frowning at the cup in his hands. Smelling the liquid inside the mug, he asks, "Did I...?"

"A vision," his mother replies. "A dark one." Something flickers in her eyes as she looks from me to Kole. Her gaze lands on my neck, then she returns her focus to her son.

Kole closes his eyes, almost like he's admitting the truth to her. In reply, she simply tilts her head to the side and smiles knowingly at him.

Watching the two of them, it's as if they're speaking their own language. A language of few words. Thessaly strokes Kole's face, then presses her forehead to his.

"I've been waiting for you," she says. "I knew it would be soon." Kole's about to answer her when she sits back and gestures to his drink. "Finish your tea, then we'll talk." She stands, then turns to take in the rest of us. When her eyes land on me, a strange sort of smile parts her lips. "Nova," she breathes. She tilts her head. "I saw you with red hair."

Self-consciously, I tuck my hair behind my ear. "It used to be. It changed when I..." I trail off because Thessaly is nodding as if she already knows what I'm about to say.

"You all look tired. I'll fetch some real tea, and some food. Then we'll talk." She pauses at the entrance. Without turning around, she says, "We have a lot to talk about."

* * *

When Thessaly returns, we eat and drink in silence. A comfortable, warm silence that makes me feel sleepy and safe. When we're finished, a young girl appears to clear our bowls and mugs, then dips back out of the tent.

"Mother?" Kole looks physically pained as he sits up straight. "You know why we're here."

Thessaly nods. "I do."

"Are you able to help us?" he asks.

I watch them carefully. He must have a million things to ask her, yet he doesn't.

"I hope so." Thessaly stands slowly. Behind her, from a large trunk, she takes out a pile of clothes. "You should all change into these," she says. "We don't have much time, and there's a lot you must see."

"We need fancy dress for that?" Luther asks sarcastically.

Kole shoots him a dark stare, but his mother simply smiles. "Yes, for the spell we're about to attempt, you do."

28

MACK

When we're dressed in our new clothes, looking like extras from a period drama, Thessaly returns. Sitting back down, she gestures for us to do the same then reaches behind her and pulls a large leather-bound book into her lap. Kole narrows his eyes.

"You remember this book?" Thessaly asks him.

"*The Origins of Magick,*" he says.

"My school had something similar." I hold out my hands. Thessaly presses the book into them. I turn to Nova as she leans in to see. Her fingers brush mine when she opens the cover.

She frowns and runs her index finger over the title, inked in elaborate lettering at the top of the first page. Below it is a story I know by heart alongside drawings I studied as a kid.

"I can't read it." Nova turns to me.

"It's written in *Mageia*—the language of our spells," Thessaly says softly.

I narrow my eyes at her. "What does this book have to do with the prophecy?"

"It's not in the book," Kole says. "The prophecy isn't old enough."

Breathing in deeply, Thessaly fixes her eyes on her son. She places a smooth hand on his shoulder. "You're right, The Phoenix Prophecy isn't in the book," she says. "But the reason for its existence is." Thessaly closes her eyes for a moment. When she opens them, she says, "Kole, Mack, Tanner, Luther —the four of you are mages. You grew up in our world. You know the story of The Original Six."

I breathe in sharply. Tanner and Luther are nodding. Kole is stock still.

As Sam slips his hand into Nova's, she stares down at the pen and ink pictures in the book. "The Original Six?" she asks, stroking the ridges of the parchment.

I look at Thessaly and she nods at me, folding her arms in front of her stomach and sitting back on her heels as if she's waiting for me to take over.

Tentatively, trying to explain while—at the same time— keeping the information as succinct as possible, I tell Nova, "Our history is divided into two eras. *The Days of Mageia* and *The Days After The Six.*"

Nova tilts her head. Her eyes fix on mine.

"*The Days of Mageia* were the early days of magick. Dark, pure magicks. As humanity changed, magick faded." I glance at Thessaly. *The Original Six.* Something about that story is important. I breathe in slowly and push my fingers through my hair. Sam and Nova grew up outside the magickal community, so they do not know the stories. They do not know their own history.

I tap the book and draw Nova's gaze to the images on the first page. "In the early 1600s, witches had forgotten how to be witches. Supers were living in the shadows. Magick was all but dead and buried."

"But humans set it free," Luther growls. His jaw pulses as he looks down at his hands.

I nod slowly. "Legend says *The Days After The Six* began in a small town. There was a woman. A young, beautiful woman called Ava. And this young woman fell in love." I pause. A heavy, twisting sensation in the pit of my stomach tells me Nova shouldn't have to hear this. I remember listening to the tale as a child and feeling such overwhelming sadness that it brought tears to my eyes.

Luther cuts in. "Ava fell in love, but not just with one man. She loved several... five to be exact." His eyes narrow. Is he thinking the same as me? *Fated to Five.*

Nova is watching him closely. Sam edges nearer to her.

Taking over for Luther, Thessaly says, "The men Ava loved were like brothers. They loved her as fiercely as she loved them, and they loved each other like brothers. But the town couldn't accept their love. People started to talk and they were cruel. Ava feared for her safety and her reputation. So, when she fell pregnant, she knew she had to marry."

"She had to choose?" Nova presses her lips together, her eyes grazing ours as she looks at each of us in turn. "How could she? If she loved them all?"

"She chose the father of her baby." Thessaly points at the book. "They married in the town's chapel. For a while, everything was well. But she couldn't help the way she felt about the other men. The six of them began their love affair once again, but they were caught. A few months after her child was born, a town gossip saw them lying with one another, all six of them."

Unexpectedly, Luther stands up. He braces his hands on the back of his head and turns away.

"What happened?" Nova asks quietly.

"They burned her," Luther replies, his words barely a whisper. When he turns around, he fixes his eyes on Nova's.

"They accused her of being a witch, they burned her at the stake, and they made her lovers watch."

For a moment, Nova doesn't move. Then she looks at Sam. He breathes out hard and pushes his fingers through his hair. "I knew about the witch trials," he said. "But I've never heard this story before."

"It's not a story," Thessaly says quietly. "It is *history*." She folds her hands in her lap and looks at Nova. "The day Ava was killed, the force of her lovers' pain unleashed the magick that had been lost to us. The elements broke free. The town was ravaged by fire, flood, cyclone, and earthquakes. But this only fueled the town's hatred and their desperation to kill anyone they suspected of witchcraft." Thessaly gestures for Nova to turn the page. On the next, there is little text, just an illustration showing burned buildings, people fleeing, and a dark broken sky. "The town destroyed itself and all the people in it." She inhales slowly and closes her eyes. "But magick was reborn. Slowly, it began its climb back into the light."

"It took a long time," Luther says, finally turning back to face us.

"Hundreds of years," Thessaly says. "But it *did* come back. Thanks to Ava and her men."

There is silence for a moment, then Nova says, "There were six of them." She is studying the image in front of her, tracing the lines with her index finger. "The prophecy says The Phoenix is fated to five." She snaps her eyes up to meet Thessaly's. Waving at the book, she says, "Are we connected to this? Is The Phoenix Prophecy connected to this story?"

A slow smile twitches Thessaly's lips. She dips her chin to her chest. "Yes," she says. "And it's time I showed you how."

29

NOVA

Thessaly takes a small black pouch from her dress. She stands, reaches inside it, and lifts her palm. Waving her hand over the flames, she sprinkles a fine silver dust into them. They crack, and fizz, and suddenly they're not orange anymore—they're black.

"Take one another's hands," she says quietly. "You must experience this together." Then she ducks back out of the tent, leaving us alone.

Slowly, I reach for Mack. He curls his large fingers around mine. With my other hand, I take hold of Sam's. Luther is the last link. When he sits down between Kole and Tanner, he hesitates. Then he looks at me, swallows hard, and holds out his hands for theirs.

The second the circle is complete, the flames disappear. Everything disappears. I'm surrounded by nothing but blackness. I close my eyes as a rushing sound fills my ears.

When I open them, I'm standing in a field full of yellow flowers. The sun is shining bright in the sky. I look up and shield my eyes; not a single cloud blots the perfect blue above me. A bird flies overhead. A hawk or a falcon. It calls out, its wings stretched wide, riding on a current of air.

Someone touches my shoulder. A young man. Barely older than twenty. He has floppy brown hair and a beautiful smile. I know him. How do I know him? As he tucks a strand of hair behind my ear and kisses my cheek, I laugh. Heat warms my cheeks.

"You make a beautiful bride, Ava."

His voice. I know his voice. But why is he calling me *Ava?* "Thank you, Tanner." I slot my hand into his. Our fingers weave together.

His gaze lingers for a moment on my face, then he reaches behind his back and says, "I have something for you." He tells me to close my eyes, then presses something into my hands.

I open my eyes. I'm holding a crown made of leaves, white roses, and feathers. I brush my fingers over the feathers' tips, then smell the roses. "Did you make this?"

Tanner smiles. "For you." He takes it back and says, "May I?"

I dip my head, so he can place the crown on top of it. Then he puts his hand on the small of my back and leads me toward a slowly moving stream.

"I told you you're a beautiful bride." He stands next to me as I look down at my shimmering reflection.

My hair is different. It's auburn—the way it used to be— and there's a flash of freckles on my nose. Yet, my face is the same. My eyes are the same.

"Are you ready?" Tanner trails a finger down my arm.

"Ready." I rest my head on his shoulder. He kisses my forehead. "Promise me nothing will change." I stand back and look up at him.

He leans down and brushes his lips on mine. Not a kiss; a whisper of a kiss. "Nothing will change. We'll still be together, but it has to happen this way." His eyes dart down to my stomach. "It's what people expect." He lowers his voice. "And with the way things are, for a while at least, the six of us need to get a bit better at playing by the rules." A smile twitches on his lips. "Or *seeming* to play by the rules."

I nod and squeeze his hand. "I know you're right. I just don't want to lose you. Any of you."

"You won't." Tanner pushes his shoulders back. He's wearing a white shirt, loose and billowy, with dark brown pants and tan boots. He lets go of me and puts his hands into his pockets. "I'll see you at the chapel."

When he's gone, I wait alone by the stream. I close my eyes and listen to the sound of the water. Something familiar is in the distance. A waterfall. I hug my arms around my waist, then look down at my clothes. I'm wearing a dress. Deep, forest green with a white blouse beneath it that peeks up over the neckline. I smooth my hands over my hips. They graze my stomach.

I look up at the sky again before following the river away from the meadow. A little way down a lane sheltered by trees, I emerge on a sloping path that leads up toward a collection of buildings. Some wood. Some stone. Ducking down an alleyway, my shoes crunch on uneven ground. Now I'm walking down a wide street. A horse and cart trots noisily past me. At the end of the street sits a chapel. White with a steepled roof.

Walking toward it, I feel as though people are whispering, staring, stopping to follow me with their eyes. I smooth my dress again and try not to look at them.

When I reach the chapel, I pause outside its large wooden doors. I wait a moment. Then the doors open.

A tall, silver-haired man with a neat beard greets me. He smiles, glances behind me, then ushers me inside. We're standing in what feels like a porch. Another door is in front of us. The hum of people's chatter tells me there's a congregation on the other side.

"You're beautiful." The man allows his fingers to brush mine. In his other hand, he's holding a bouquet of flowers. As our skin meets, my breath catches in my chest. His eyes sparkle as he presses the bouquet into my hands. "Are you ready?"

I nod and loop my arm in his.

As we enter the body of the chapel—small, dark, and wooden—the sea of people in front of us turns around. They watch as I walk slowly toward the minister, my arm tucked into the arm of the man with the sparkling eyes. When we reach the front of the chapel, the minister turns to the man and says, "Rhone Mackenzie, you are here because you wish to give your charge over to be married?"

A shiver grips my spine. *Mack.*

"I am." Mack unhooks his arm from mine and stands with his arms behind his back, fingers laced together, feet apart.

"The name of the man who shall take your charge as his wife?" The minister is looking past me.

I turn and follow his gaze. First, I see Tanner. He's at the far end of the front pew, sitting with his hands braced on his knees. He smiles at me, then looks down at the floor. Next to him, a guy with dark, curly hair. He looks down at the floor too.

My eyes move along the line. There is a large gap, filled with two plump women who have large lips and long blond hair. Then another figure I recognize. Tall like a Viking, with a long dark beard, this man does not look at the floor—he looks straight at me as if he's trying to see inside my soul.

"Luther Ross." Mack speaks loudly. His words bounce off the chapel walls and seem to fill it up.

I look away from the Viking. Next to him, a man with thick, black hair is staring at his hands. They are knotted together in his lap. He raises his head. Something flashes in his eyes. *Luther.*

Fixing his eyes on me, Luther stands. He steps forward and moves to my right while Mack stands on my left. With both of them next to me, I feel suddenly safer. More at ease.

"Very well." The minister nods at Mack. "Rhone, you may take a seat."

Mack dips his head, then pats my shoulder and takes Luther's place in the pew behind us.

When I look at Luther, something swells in my chest. Excitement. Happiness. *Love.* He smiles at me. It brightens his face.

"Luther Ross," the minister raises his voice, "will you take this woman as your wedded wife?"

"I will." Luther takes my hands. His fingers are warm. He strokes my palm with his thumb.

"Ava Sparrow, will you take this man as your wedded husband?" The minister's eyes narrow as he waits for my reply.

"Yes," I say. "I will."

NOVA

I t is dark. A fire crackles in the grate. I am lying on a sheepskin rug, a blanket draped over me. Hanging from a hook by the fire is the crown Tanner made for me. I study it as a hand traces the curve of my back. I turn and look up into the face of my husband.

Luther strokes my hair from my face. He kisses my temple, my cheek, my mouth. His hands slide down my body. He pulls the blanket aside, then lowers his lips and peppers my stomach with a row of kisses.

I close my eyes and push my fingers through his thick, beautiful hair. "I can't wait for you to meet her."

He looks up at me. His eyes dance with pleasure. "You're certain it's a *her*?"

I nod and smile at him. "Certain." I tweak my index finger beneath his chin and pull him up toward me. "And I'm certain that you will be a wonderful father."

IT'S DAYLIGHT. I'm in the meadow. My stomach is bigger. Luther's arms wrap tightly around my waist, but someone else is there too. Tanner appears at Luther's shoulder. He leans over and kisses me. For a moment, I resist. My heart thumps in my chest. "Someone could see," I tell him.

"We're alone," he says.

"We're alone," Luther repeats, then turns us around and nudges me into Tanner's waiting arms. As Luther moves my hair aside and kisses the back of my neck, Tanner kisses my lips.

The three of us sink to the ground.

* * *

EMBERS GLOW IN THE FIREPLACE. A full moon shines down through the window. I'm lying on the rug, on my side. Luther is standing in front of me. Naked. He wraps his fingers around his shaft and runs his tongue along his lower lip.

Hands that aren't Luther's arrive on my hip. I lean back. Tanner kisses me. He cups my breasts, skims his hand over my stomach, eases my legs open. When I push back toward him, he's hard. His erection presses against me. He finds my pussy, readies me with his fingers, then slides his cock inside.

He moves slowly, patiently. I rock against him. Luther kneels down and brings his shaft to my lips. At the same time, I realize we're not alone.

"Be gentle with her, Kole," Luther growls.

The Viking nods. His eyes flash as he looks at me from farther down the rug. "I promise." He lowers his head. His teeth graze my inner thigh, then his tongue slides over my clit.

"Here…" Another voice. I return to Luther's waiting cock. Mack is kneeling beside him. He strokes my face, then holds my mouth open as Luther slowly inches into it.

As Tanner moves inside me and Kole's tongue swirls pleasure into my core, I hum and groan.

In the corner of the room, someone else watches us. "Can I...?" The dark-haired boy. Not a boy—a young man like Tanner. He stands and walks over to us. He crouches on the other side of Luther.

"She needs your mouth, Sam." Tanner brushes his thumb over my nipple. "Here, put your mouth here."

I close my eyes and let the five of them fill me up. Fill me with feeling, and fire, and thunder. When I come, my orgasm makes the walls shudder.

* * *

LUTHER IS NEXT TO ME. He's holding my hand. In front of us, a baby lies in a crib. She makes a small mewing sound. A tear rolls down my cheek.

"I told you she'd be a girl." I turn to Luther. He's crying, too.

"You two make good babies," Tanner says, rubbing my shoulder.

"She's beautiful, Ava." Mack is standing on the other side of the crib. "Well done."

* * *

IT'S PITCH DARK. The baby is sleeping. I get up and pad across the cold floor to check on her. I'm about to lift her out and bring her into bed with me and Luther, to keep her warm, when I hear something outside.

Luther sits up.

A fist bangs our door. It rattles on its hinges. "Ava, Luther, open up."

I clutch the baby to my chest and inch back toward the

wall. Luther stands and reaches for his knife, positioning himself in front of me.

The door clatters inward. The flicker of torchlight fills the room.

"They're alone," someone says.

"I saw them." A woman steps forward and jabs her finger in our direction. "I saw them before the baby was born. The six of them. Doing *unspeakable* things."

I shake my head. Fear grips my limbs.

"They're always here. The two boys, the tall one, and Rhone." She spits on the ground. "She's got them under her spell."

Luther moves to charge forward but then the minister appears. He puts his arms out and shakes his head. "Luther, we just want to talk to Ava."

"Rhone was her patron. Her godfather. She *seduced* him. She seduced all of them!" The woman is almost screaming now. Someone else yells, too. Then another, and another.

"Witch! She's a witch!"

My blood runs cold. I hold the baby closer. My heart thunders so hard I can barely hear anymore. The baby starts to cry. I shake my head. "Please, stop, you're scaring her."

"Get out of my house." Luther waves his knife, but then someone charges forward. A man with white-blond hair. He grabs Luther by the throat, knocks the knife to the ground, then kicks him in the stomach so he falls to his knees.

"Put the baby down." The minister gestures to the crib.

At first, I can't move. I *won't* move. But then he meets my eyes.

"If you fight us, Ava, we'll have to assume we're right. If you come peacefully and talk to us, there might be a way out of this for you."

I'm trembling from head to toe. I lower the baby into her crib. A sob wracks my chest. My ribs tighten. My lungs feel like they will explode. Two more men stride into the house and grab my arms.

As they march me away, I call, "Luther, whatever happens, take care of our baby! You take *care* of our baby!"

* * *

THE SUN IS SETTING. I stare at it. The light hurts my eyes. My ears are buzzing, but something breaks through. A crackling sound. I realize my legs are warm. Not just warm... hot. I look down. Flames lick my feet. They're bare and dirty. I try to move them, but they're tied at the ankles.

I tug my arms. They're tied too.

Someone is screaming. I raise my eyes away from my burning feet. My chest is tight. I cough. My eyes begin to water. I blink the moisture away. A crowd is gathered in front of me. I find Tanner first. He is holding the baby. I smile at him. She looks happy in his arms. Peaceful. Next to him, Sam is trembling.

Kole and Mack are restraining Luther. He is the one who is screaming. He tries to lunge forward, but there are men with swords. They raise their weapons. One of them slashes at Luther's shirt. He starts to bleed but doesn't seem to notice or to care.

"You can't do this!" He screams.

This time, the man who cut him punches him hard. He goes limp. Kole and Mack are the only things holding him up. As blood trickles down Luther's face, he falls to his knees.

"Ava Ross has been found guilty of using dark magick," a voice booms. Not the minister. Someone else. He's holding a large piece of parchment and reading from it. "She bewitched five of our men. She denied her crimes. For this, she will burn."

The crowd cheers. Someone throws something but it

doesn't reach me; it lands in the embers and sends sparks flying up in front of my face.

Heat is creeping up my legs now. Gnawing at my clothes. Licking them from my body.

Mack leaves Luther's side and pleads with the man holding the parchment. "Please, you don't have to do this."

"Rhone, we have known each other a long time." The man squeezes Mack's arm. "I'm doing this for you, my friend." He looks past Mack at the others. "For all of you. When the witch is gone, you will be free."

Another scream fills my ears. It's different this time; higher pitched, more like a wail. It reverberates through my bones. As pain threatens to crack me open, I realize it's me. I am the one screaming.

The last thing I see before the flames swallow me up is the faces of the five men I love. Their hearts are breaking, and mine breaks, too.

Luther calls my name.

I close my eyes. I listen to his voice.

Pain devours me.

LUTHER

A cyclone of black fire rushes up to the top of the tent. It blasts a hole in the roof. The canvas catches light. Flames snake down toward the struts. Someone is tugging on my arm.

"Luther, we have to go." Kole shakes me. He's crouching in front of me. He pulls me to my feet. Tanner's firing water at the flames, but they're not diminishing. I push Kole away from me. My chest is tight. I can't breathe, but it's not because of the fire or the smoke. It's the pain. Squeezing my ribs. Crushing my lungs.

Once out of the tent, I stumble away from the heat. Into the trees. Into the dark. Then I fall to my knees. Grief threatens to break me in half. I bend over, grasp the earth, feel it beneath my fingers, but it doesn't ground me. I'm still there. I still see her burning. I still smell it, feel it, taste it.

There's a hand on my shoulder. A warm hand. *Her* hand.

"Luther?" Nova's face appears in front of mine. Her hair is still silver, but for a moment I see red. Auburn. Freckles on the bridge of her nose. Her eyes—one brown, one blue.

She strokes my face. My cheeks are wet.

I try to speak but the words catch in my throat. I screw my eyes shut. I see her in the chapel with flowers in her hair. I see my hands on her stomach.

"Look at me, Luther." Nova presses her forehead to mine then sits back. When I finally open my eyes, she cups my face with her hands. "You saw," she says. A statement not a question.

"I saw you. I saw us." I clasp her fingers with mine. "You were my wife." The words break as they leave my mouth. "I was your husband."

Nova is crying too. Big, thick tears roll down her cheeks. I sink into her chest. Her heart is beating. I can hear it. She's here, but I still feel like I lost her.

"I'm sorry I left you," she says quietly. Barely a whisper. "I'm sorry I broke your heart."

As she speaks, the sadness in my lungs shifts into something else. I sit up and stare into her eyes. "It wasn't your fault." I push my fingers through her hair and pull her face closer to mine. "It wasn't your fault." I brush her lower lip with my thumb. Her mouth opens. A small whimper escapes.

I close my eyes and bring her to me. I wrap her in my arms and kiss her deeply, my tongue seeking hers. Pulling her into my lap, I run my hands up her back. She's not close enough. I need her closer.

Her arms are around my neck. She shrugs off the shawl Thessaly gave her. It drops to the floor. I pull the string at the front of her dress. It falls open, exposing the tops of her breasts. I run my tongue along them. I kiss a line up to her throat. Her head jerks back and she groans as I tug the dress lower.

Her nipples are hard in the cold night air. I pull one small pink bud into my mouth and swirl my hot tongue over it. Nova grinds her hips forward, pushing her core down onto my erection. She lifts my head from her chest and looks into my eyes.

"You hated me because you loved me," she whispers, stroking my lips. "You were angry with me because I left you. We loved each other. So much."

I close my eyes. Images pummel my brain. Another me. Another her. Another life. So much love. "I never hated you." I smooth her hair back over her shoulders.

"Prove it." Nova reaches for my belt. She unfastens it quickly and lifts herself up as she pulls my erection free. I put my hands under her dress, then move her panties aside and guide my shaft to her pussy.

Holding myself tightly, I stroke her clit with the head of my cock. She fumbles with my buttons, slides her hands beneath my shirt, then leans down and gently bites my shoulder.

She's about to lower herself onto me when I grab her hips and stop her. She meets my eyes. "I want to watch your face as I enter you."

Nova licks her lower lip. She kisses my forehead, then my cheeks, my jaw, my neck. She keeps my gaze as she slides down onto me. Her heat envelops my length, squeezing it tight. She brings my hands to her back, and I hold her close— so close I can barely tell where she ends and I begin.

When I rock up into her, she grinds down in return. She murmurs something into my ear, but I don't hear her. She moans and wraps her legs around me, easing me deeper inside.

The first time we fucked, it was urgent, angry, fevered. We scratched and bit and pounded an orgasm out of each other. Last night on the train, it was over in seconds. A dirty explosion of heat. This time, our orgasms build slowly. Like a storm. Air pulsing, pressure increasing, ready for thunder to rumble through us and for lightning to strike.

I move slowly inside her, changing the direction of my hips, watching her eyes widen and the color rush to her cheeks as she clings onto me. She runs her hands up my chest. She skims her hands over my arms, laces her fingers around my neck, and moans into my mouth when I kiss her.

I tilt backward and reach between us, finding her clit and playing with it until her breath quickens and her back arches. As she starts to come, I wrap my arms around her. Her walls pulse. My cock swells. My body stiffens. The orgasm washes over me. Over my whole body. This time, it's not quick or dirty—it's long, lingering. It takes my breath away and sends waves of heat through my core.

When I press my forehead to hers, Nova whispers, "I missed you. I won't leave you again. I promise."

NOVA

"Nova?" Thessaly's tall silhouette appears in the trees behind us. I stand and adjust my dress, but I don't feel embarrassed. Luther stands too, keeping close to me.

"The tent?" I look back through the trees, trying to spot signs of an out-of-control fire.

"Tanner put out the flames." Thessaly steps forward, so we can see her face. "Are the two of you alright?" She tilts her head to the side as she waits for our answer.

"Did you know?" Luther grasps my hand. He's staring at Thessaly with fire in his eyes. "What we were going to see?"

Slowly, Thessaly nods. "I knew." She gestures back toward the tents. "Come. I'm sure you have many questions."

When we reach the clearing, Kole and the others are standing in a circle talking quietly. He's the first to see me.

Little Star. His voice fills me up. It makes me want to cry.

In unison, the five of them envelop me. I can't tell who is kissing me or who's hands are who's. I don't know where I begin and they end. All I know is that even though nothing makes sense, at the same time, it does.

"This way." Thessaly gestures to a larger tent with feathers strung outside it. She ducks inside and we follow her.

As we gather around another fire, she lifts a small iron kettle and hangs it over the flames.

Kole smooths his hands over his hair as he looks at his mother. "What we just saw, it wasn't just a story was it?" I've never seen him so pale. "We were there. It was *us*?"

Next to Kole, Tanner has closed his eyes—as if he's trying to block out the whirlpool of emotions filling the tent.

Thessaly sits down, crossed legged, and motions for us to do the same.

I shake my head. "I can't sit." I flex my fingers, fold my arms, then unfold them. "I need to know what that was... what did we see?"

Again, Thessaly nods for us to sit down. When the others obey, even Luther, I give in and lower myself to my knees. He sits opposite me, staring at me through the flames. I put my hands on my thighs and lean onto them. "Was it real?" My words catch in my throat. "What we saw? What we *felt*? Was it real?"

"It was real." Tanner's voice is shaky. He rubs his neck and mutters, "So much pain."

Pressing her lips together, Thessaly inhales slowly. "I'm sorry you had to go through that," she says. "All of you. But you needed to feel it. You needed to understand."

"I don't understand." I shake my head. "I *don't* understand."

"Yes," Thessaly says, smiling at me, "you do." She presses her hand to her chest. "What does your heart tell you, Nova?"

Before I can answer, Kole looks across at his mother. "We were here before," he says, an answer not a question. "The six of us. We have been here before."

Thessaly locks eyes with him. She tilts her head to the

side. A braid escapes from behind her ear and falls in front of her cheek. "Yes," she says, "and no." She looks at each of us in turn. "The six of you are descendants of The Original Six. The things you just experienced happened to your ancestors hundreds of years ago. You are their descendants."

As Mack breathes out a heavy sigh, Sam laughs a little. He scrapes his fingers through his hair and shakes his head. "That's crazy. Wouldn't you guys have known? Wouldn't your families have known?"

"Not necessarily," Mack says. "The records are vague. No one even knew their names. It was just a story." He sucks in his cheeks and flexes his fingers as if he's trying to make himself think straight. "It was just a story." When he looks up, he turns to Thessaly. "Have you always known?"

Reaching for him, squeezing his hand tightly in the first display of true emotion since we got here, Thessaly says, "No. Not always." She fixes her eyes on Kole's. "I had my first vision about The Six when you were just a baby. I knew you'd be important."

"And you were the one who was sent The Phoenix Prophecy?" Mack asks in a tone that makes me feel as if he's about to get out his cop notebook.

Thessaly nods. "It was sent to me when Kole was five years old. At the time, there were no official records of the prophecies that seers received. We simply kept them in our heads and acted on them if they became relevant." She glances at Mack. "When the Bureau introduced the Prophecies Archive, I handed it over."

Mack frowns. He, Luther, and Kole all look shocked at Thessaly's revelation. "You handed it over?" Mack says. "That's not possible. There was no record of The Phoenix Prophecy until Kole accessed it for The League."

Before Thessaly can answer, I nudge Mack's arm. "Annalise said the Bureau has been infiltrated by The League.

What if it started way before we thought? What if *that's* how Ragnor and his demon friend knew about the prophecy? Because someone at the Bureau stole it?"

Mack shakes his head. "Ragnor didn't know what it said. That's why they needed Kole. They couldn't access it. All they knew was that it existed."

There's a pause, in which I can almost hear the guys' thoughts whirring in their brains. Then Thessaly clears her throat and says, "They couldn't access it because I protected it."

In unison, we turn to look at her.

"I cast an incantation, so that if the prophecy was ever passed to someone outside the Bureau, it would destroy itself. I also... paraphrased a little." She moistens her lower lip. "The version I gave to the Bureau said simply that a girl would be born with the power to stop the underworld rising. I left out the details." She shrugs and reaches for the kettle. "What can I say? I don't trust authority figures."

As Thessaly sets out seven copper cups, and pours hot brown liquid into them, I rub my temples. They're throbbing. The sensation trickles down into my veins, like pain, and fear, and terror from the vision are still living inside me.

We each take a cup of tea. I blow across the top of mine, then take a long sip. Whatever it's made of it smells heavenly and it eases the throbbing in my head.

Mack is the first to speak. Slowly, as if he's thinking very carefully, tying the pieces together and watching them fit, he taps the side of his cup. "So, you gave the Bureau an edited version of The Phoenix Prophecy. Someone at the Bureau stole it, but it destroyed itself, and all they learned was that some girl, somewhere, was destined to stop the underworld rising."

No one says anything. Setting his cup down, Mack stands

up and we simply watch him as he begins to pace up and down, hands behind his back.

"And the six of us are part of The Phoenix Prophecy because we are descendants of The Original Six."

Thessaly stands now, too. The bracelets on her wrist jangle as they knock against one another. She puts her hand on Mack's elbow, then turns to look at the rest of us. "The love your ancestors shared was so powerful, and the pain of their loss so great, that it passed through the generations." She pauses and looks up at the ceiling of the tent as tears fill her eyes. She wipes them then shakes her head. "When your ancestors watched Ava die, something was set in motion. Something that changed the history of magick and the supernatural world. Other witches were burned. Some had magickal powers, some were just women who did not behave the way society wanted them to behave." She breathes in deeply. "But instead of extinguishing magick, the people who burned those witches set something free. They released our power. Magick didn't die—it grew. No matter how hard they tried to stamp it out." She takes in the six of us. "It took a long time for you all to find each other again. The essence of The Original Six passed through generation after generation. It was dormant for centuries. But that is how it had to be. You were destined to be reunited when the time was right."

"Now is the right time?" I ask, holding my cup so tightly my knuckles whiten. "Because of Ragnor?"

Thessaly blinks at me. "Yes, Nova. Because of what Ragnor is about to unleash."

"You've seen it? What he's trying to set free?" I ask, wrapping my arms around my waist as a cold breeze whips through the closed tent door.

Thessaly nods. "Yes."

"But you've seen us stopping it?" Kole dips his head to meet his mother's eyes.

For a moment, just a flash of a moment, something passes between the two of them. I can't read it. It's too fast, but it makes my skin prickle with uncertainty.

Without answering Kole's question, Thessaly says, "There is only one more thing I can tell you."

I glance at Mack. He's staring intently at Thessaly.

"The town," she says. "Its name was not recorded. Of all the texts we have, not a single one mentions its name." She breathes out heavily and rubs her knees then, fixing her gaze on mine, she whispers, "Where ashes turn to light."

A blanket of ice creeps down my spine. A memory flashes in front of my eyes. A green sign. Late at night. At the side of the road. "Phoenix Falls?"

Thessaly nods slowly.

I turn to look at the others. All but Sam look practically gray with shock. Kole shakes his head. "How did we not know?" He laughs ironically and repeats himself, looking at Mack. "We believed Phoenix Falls was important but how did we not know about this?"

Before Mack can answer, Thessaly says, "There's one more thing." Tentatively, she turns to Mack. "Many bad things have happened at The Hollow."

I frown, studying Mack's face. Is Thessaly talking about Layla?

"Mack," she says, "The Hollow was built on the remains of the original town square." She swallows hard. "The witches who were burned were buried in its grounds."

As a shiver rocks my body, I hear Tanner whisper, "Fuck."

Mack doesn't say anything. He's barely moving. His breath is so shallow in his chest that I can hardly see it. When I look at his hand, it's shaking. I reach for him and squeeze his fingers with mine.

He looks at me as if he's surprised I'm speaking to him. "The Hollow..." He takes his hand back and pushes his fingers through his hair. To Thessaly, he says, "All the bad things that have happened there. The energy beneath it… that's why Ragnor has to perform the ritual there."

Thessaly sits back on her heels and presses her hands together, almost as if she's praying. "Yes," she says. "Yes, that's why."

Silence descends on the group. My skin is fizzing, my chest tight, my heart aching as memories that aren't mine flash behind my eyes. I see my men, standing in front of me. I feel fire at my feet. I see a small bundle of rags, held tight in Luther's arms. Our daughter.

I study each of the guys in turn, hoping just one of them might look like they're together enough to tell me it's all going to be all right. But the stories etched on their faces tell me we're all feeling the same thing—shock, pain, grief.

Rising slowly, Thessaly pads quietly to the entrance of the tent. "I have given you all I can," she says, her hand grazing Kole's shoulder as she passes him. "What happens next is for the six of you to decide."

She pauses, as if she's about to say something else, then simply sighs heavily and leaves us alone.

As I draw my knees up under my chin and hug them tight to my body, Tanner pours more tea from the iron kettle. Mack opens Thessaly's book and starts to pore over its words. Luther announces he needs to go for a walk. I'm about to stop him when Kole raises his palm at me. "He needs a minute, Little Star."

I glance at Tanner. He squeezes my hand. "Luther was your *husband*, Nova. You had a child together."

At the word 'child', a tsunami of tears rattles my chest. I screw my eyes shut and let Tanner hold me while I sob. When the crying ends, and Tanner presses a mug of tea into my hands, I try to feel something. Anything. I've gone from being overwhelmed by emotion to almost completely numb. Dragging my thoughts from Ava's memories, which are still assaulting my brain, I ask quietly, "That's why we're supposed to save the world? The six of us? Because we loved each other, and our love can make powerful magick?" I laugh a little and shake my head. "I just don't see how…"

"You didn't feel it." Luther's voice makes me turn around. He's back, standing in the doorway of the tent. When he ducks inside and sits down next to Kole, he looks at me across the fire. "You died. You were gone. You didn't feel it. How it was for us."

I open my mouth to reply, then realize he's right. My vision ended when the flames engulfed me. But perhaps they saw more than that.

"It broke us," Sam says quietly.

The expressions on their faces make my throat tighten with tears. Love swells in my chest. The way I love the five of them bleeds into the way Ava loved her men. It fills me up until there's no room left inside me because I'm carrying her feelings and mine and, surely, one person can't *feel* this much.

"Is this what it feels like in your head?" I turn to Mack and tap my temple. "Is this what it's like to have two different sets of thoughts and feelings living in your head all the time? The same but different? Yours but not yours? Because, right now, I have no idea where my feelings end and Ava's begin."

Mack's lips twitch. Without answering me, he puts down the book and brings me into his lap, cradling me against his chest. I sigh and breathe him in. After several long moments of silence, Sam is the one who speaks up.

"What do we do now?" he asks, knees up against his chest, arms wrapped around them. "We know *why* we're part of the prophecy, but how does this help us?" When no one answers, he repeats, "How does this help us defeat Ragnor? Because he's almost ready. He's going to bring Elena back to life, and he's going to give The Shadow King Nova's name. So, how does this help us?"

33

MACK

I t doesn't fucking help. Not one bit. Sure, it's nice to know why we're part of the prophecy and where Nova's power comes from. It might help *me* to know that my sister killed herself because The Hollow was damned to hell from the moment we set foot in it. Laced with evil. Dripping with darkness.

But Sam's right; it does fuck-all to help us defeat Ragnor.

Kole can tell I'm angry. He rubs his knees, stands up, and says, "I'm going to speak to my mother. I'll be back." Then he disappears outside.

Usually, I do my best to stay calm. To be the responsible one who analyses a situation and comes up with answers. But right now I am anything but calm.

"Mack?" Nova puts her hand on my chest, like she can feel me vibrating beneath her and wants to calm me.

"I need a minute." I stand up, sliding her off my lap, and stumble outside. I'm barely into the trees when Snow takes over. It happens quickly. More quickly than normal.

We stand, shaking, breathing hard, hot breath puffing out from our large black nose.

Then we stand on our hind legs and roar. It shakes the trees and the ground. It makes birds fly from their branches. But it doesn't dampen the pain.

Layla's face races through our head. How many times did she tell us she was sad, but that she had no idea why? How many times did she beg our parents to leave The Hollow? How many times did she tell us she had nightmares that stayed long after she woke?

Shoving our recently dislocated shoulder hard into a nearby tree, we yowl in pain. It hurts like fuck, but we deserve it. We should have listened to her.

We're ramming our huge, muscular body into the trunk again, and again, and again when Nova finds us. She stands just beyond the shadow of the trees and waits.

Slowly, we latch onto her presence. When we finally stop thrusting our already-injured shoulder into the tree, and stand barely able to breathe, she comes to us. She weaves her fingers into our fur, then strokes our face. We lean into her. Snow is almost purring.

"You couldn't have known," she whispers. "You couldn't have protected Layla because you couldn't have known."

And, with that, our heart breaks all over again.

WHEN WE RETURN to the tent, I'm myself again and Nova is holding my hand. The others look up. With no clothes at hand, I grab a blanket and wrap it around my waist. Without speaking, as I sit next to him, Luther puts a firm hand on my shoulder. He knows my past. Apart from Sam, they all do.

"Nova will explain later," I tell him.

"You don't have to tell me anything," Sam says.

"You're one of us," I reply, meeting his eyes. "We're brothers now."

"Thank you," he says. A genuine thank you, filled with sincerity.

Turning to the others, I lace my fingers together in my lap and tell them, "I'm sorry. What just happened was a lot for all of us. I shouldn't have—"

"My friend," Kole's gruff voice stops me mid-sentence. "You have nothing to apologize for. What we learned has great implications. We're *all* feeling it."

"My whole life," Tanner adds, wide eyed. "It's making me question everything. Everything I know about myself. My affinity. The things I've done." He looks longingly at Nova, as if touching her might be the only thing that could quiet his thoughts. "Was it all preordained? Written in the stars? Are we just copies of people who've been here already?"

"I don't think it works that way," Kole says. He pinches the top of his nose. "We're not the same people. The memory of their lives has been carried by our ancestors. Hidden. Buried. Now it's been awakened, it lives in us." He flexes his fingers at his sides. "I know it's hard to understand. I think the only certainty was that we'd find each other again when the time was right."

"Did your mother tell you that?" Luther asks, a hint of bitterness in his voice.

Kole doesn't answer the question. Instead, he says, "She has told us all she can. It's up to us what we do with the information we have."

As anger returns to bite at the back of my throat, Nova is the one who speaks up. "We should go back to Phoenix Falls," she says. "Nico said the ritual would take place in two days' time. We need to get back and figure out how we're going to stop it."

"I thought that was why we came here," Luther says.

"It hasn't been a waste." Nova can tell we're all deflated. "We now know that we're bound together, and that the way we feel about each other—and the way our ancestors felt—is the route of our power."

"We already knew that," Tanner mutters quietly. "The prophecy told us we were fated to you, and *all* magick draws its power from emotion."

Tilting her head, as if she's surprised Tanner is being as pessimistic as Luther, Nova says, "But we've felt it now." She looks around at each of us in turn. "We've felt the pain, the loss, the grief. We saw what they saw... The Original Six. We know they are a part of us. So, maybe that's what we needed. The key to open the floodgates. Maybe now, when we confront Ragnor, we'll be able to draw on their past strength and we'll beat him."

As Nova's gloriously naïve words sink in, Kole is the one who stands and offers her his hand. When she's on her feet, he cups her face in his hands. He doesn't speak, just stares at her for a moment.

I glance at the others, wondering if they've realized that Kole and Nova can talk without words. I knew it when they first returned from the League's clutches. The way they look at each other sometimes, the way their eyes lock and a million expressions pass over their faces, it's obvious to anyone who's ever witnessed a blood bonded couple.

"Is she right?" Sam interrupts their silent moment. He stands too, and draws himself up so he's a little taller. "Is Nova right? What we saw will set her power free?"

Kole draws in a deep breath. "We need to return to Phoenix Falls," he says. "We should sleep now. Tomorrow morning, first light, we leave for the train."

A while later, we are lying curled around the fire, Nova stretched out between Kole and Luther, when Tanner whispers to me in the darkness. "He didn't answer Sam's question, did he?"

My jaw tightens. "No," I reply. "He did not."

34

NICO

I n daylight, The Hollow is less terrifying. Eve's altar looks like a plaything. A collection of childish objects that couldn't possibly do any harm. But, of course, that's the opposite of what they are.

For days now, she's barely left the lawn of the mansion. I'm not sure if she sleeps. Her eyes are large, black, and surrounded by spidering veins and spread further down her face as the hours pass. She is high on F.H.B, that much is obvious, and she's dangerously close to losing control.

I'm watching her skip in circles around the fountain when Andre—my least favorite of Ragnor's wolves—comes outside. He looks down at me, neither friendly or unfriendly, and hands me a mug of coffee. "Wish we could fucking get on with it," he growls.

"Alignment needs to be right," I say, looking up at the pinkish morning sky. "Apparently."

"Fuck," Andre says, rolling his eyes. "She creeps me out."

Eve is now draped over the fountain, her hair spread beneath her like a halo in the water. As if she knows we are talking about her, she turns her head toward us. She curls her finger at Andre.

"You're wanted," I tell him.

Andre swallows hard but doesn't dare refuse. By the time he's reached her, Eve has pulled her dress up around her thighs. She grins, sits up, and spreads her legs. Turns out, finding her creepy isn't enough to stop Andre from fucking her.

As they start rutting against the fountain, I get up and stalk back into the house. The place is a mess, and it's hard to imagine the days when Mack and the others were here. When Nova was here with them. When she thought I was her salvation.

I glance up at the clock. I last saw them three days ago and have heard nothing since they told me to leave. Last night, it became too much. I crept back out to the cabin, but when I waited at the barrier—even when I called him—Sam didn't come. And something told me he wasn't there.

Have they run? Did they take my advice and get the fuck out of Phoenix Falls?

The thought makes me both happy and sad. I want Sam and Nova to be safe. I couldn't give a rat's ass about the others, but I want those two safe. Happy. Together. At the same time, though, the idea I might never see them again makes me want to punch a hole in the wall.

I'm about to do just that when my mother appears in the doorway. She looks exhausted, like she hasn't slept in days either. Her skin is stretched thin over her angular cheek bones, and she has dark circles beneath her eyes.

"It's happening tonight," she says, taking the coffee from my hand and downing it in one gulp. "It's finally happening. Tonight."

Icy fingers of dread grip my spine. "What will happen?" I sink down onto one of Mack's wooden chairs.

"At midnight, Eve will perform the ritual."

"To bring Elena back?" I ask, swallowing hard as Sam's face—and the way he looked when I told him our father was planning to resurrect his mother—fills my mind.

Mother shakes her head. Lowering her voice, she sits opposite me. She's cradling the empty coffee cup, staring into it as if it contains tea leaves that might give her a whisper of hope about the future. "Eve's ritual will open a portal. The Shadow King will appear. Ragnor will give him Nova's name and tell him where she is. Then the King will bring Elena back."

"And then...? The King brings his demon friends to play?"

My tone makes my mother flinch. "This isn't a game, Nico." She grabs my hands and clasps them tight between hers, her knuckles whitening with the pressure. "The King will have Nova killed, then he will return for his ascension."

"Have her killed?" I take back my hands, rubbing them to bring back some feeling. "He won't do it himself?"

Mother sighs and buries her head in her hands. "Does it matter?" she mutters. "Does any of it matter? When she's dead, the ascension can begin. When she's dead, all of this will be over."

Her tone of voice makes me shudder. I dip my head to meet her eyes. "Do you *want* it to be over?" I ask her.

There's a noise in the hallway. Footsteps, followed by Ragnor's unmistakable scent. Sitting up straight, Mother rearranges her features and smiles. "I want us to take our rightful place, Nico. With the King. Supers and demons ruling the earth together, while humans languish in pain and torment for the rest of their sorry existence."

Her tone tells me she means what she's saying; it's the same tone Ragnor uses. Defiant, vitriolic, dripping with hate. But her eyes tell me a different story—her eyes say she's just as scared as I am.

NOVA

When we wake, the atmosphere in the tent is strained. What we saw yesterday has brought us closer, but it's also weighing heavily on our shoulders. Kole, especially, seems more distant. Something happened to him in the forest before we got here, and something happened when he left to speak to his mother. We all know it, and the fact he's not sharing it with us is creating a strange unspoken tension.

"Seers have their own rules," Mack tells me as we eat bowls of stewed oats and drink hot sweet coffee. He shifts uncomfortably as he talks, his shoulder still painful after his self-flagellation in the forest yesterday. "Some are a little more relaxed these days but communes like Foresight—people like Kole and Thessaly—they take their obligations very seriously."

"What does that mean?"

Mack glances over at the empty space where Kole should be sitting. Instead, he's disappeared once again to speak to his mother. "It means there is a limit to what they can share with us. There are things they can't tell us, even if they want to."

I press my lips together. The oatmeal has settled like lead in my stomach. I put my bowl down and stick to the coffee instead. Back in my regular clothes, I feel a little more like myself. The coffee is helping, too.

"It's nuts." Sam has eaten everything in his bowl. He's now sitting cross-legged, shaking his head. "The whole thing. Who made these rules?"

Mack offers him a wry smile. "Remind me and I'll give you a lecture on it someday. Right now, we should try to be satisfied that Kole has told us all he can."

There's a pregnant pause before Sam, looking down into his coffee, says, "What about me?"

I frown at him. "What do you mean?"

"The five of you have magick. The Original Six unleashed magick on the world. We're supposed to use their energy to defeat Ragnor, right? Only, I'm not a mage. I'm a werewolf. So, what about me? What's my role in all this?" He smiles a crooked smile at me. "I guess I could be your therapy wolf. Ease your stress with some belly rubs and long walks in the forest. But I'm not sure that'll help fight the big bad."

I'm about to reply when I realize I have no idea what to say. Sam's right; he doesn't have magick. Trying to paint a light-hearted smile on my face, I tell him, "Maybe you're supposed to bite me again. Unleash my rage."

"I could bite you," Sam counters. "If you want me to." He raises an eyebrow, then puts his coffee down and crawls over to me. Planting his arms either side of me, he nips at my neck, and I fall back into Mack's lap, laughing.

"Hands off my wife," Luther growls. For a moment, I think he's serious. Until I look at his face and see the way he's watching us. With anticipation instead of anger.

Mack is unfastening the tie on the front of my dress, and

slipping his hands inside, when the tent opens and Kole strides in. He's holding our backpacks, all six of them, and stops in the entrance.

"Time to move out," he says. "Mom's got a friend in the next village who can lend us a truck."

I'm about to ask why he's decided against the train, but something in his face tells me he's not in the mood for talking.

Reluctantly, I sit up. I wanted to lose myself in them. I wanted a few minutes of feeling nothing but good things. But it looks like that'll have to wait.

IT's an hour's walk to the next village. By the time we get there, my legs are sore with the effort of walking on a steep incline in non-hiking boots.

Kole tells us to wait in the shelter of the trees and heads for a farmhouse that looks pretty much abandoned. We see no signs of movement inside, but he returns a few minutes later driving a beaten-up old truck with no plates.

"I'll drive," he says, gesturing for us to pile in.

Mack and Luther sit up front with Kole while Tanner, Sam, and I take the bench seat in the back. Our packs are in the cargo bed, covered with a large gray tarp.

We drive in silence for a while, until Luther flicks on the radio and turns it up. The noise makes me relax a little. Sandwiched between Tanner and Sam, I shuffle to get comfortable. Without me having to ask, Tanner picks up my legs and pulls them across his lap while Sam angles his chest to support my back. I hug Sam's large muscly arm and rest my head on his chest while Tanner rubs my feet.

"I kinda miss the dress," he says eventually, trailing his

eyes up my body. "I mean, you look good in anything, but things with gaping necklines are a definite win."

I roll my eyes at him and nudge his stomach with my foot. Catching it, Tanner starts to rub my calves. His hands are perfect. Large, tanned, and gorgeously strong. But instead of melting into his touch and encouraging him to slide his hands higher up my legs, before I know it, I'm asleep.

When I open my eyes again, we're in the turnout on the edge of the forest and Kole is already unloading our bags from the back of the truck. It's mid-afternoon and the forest is wrapped in warm, dappled sunlight.

Mack puts his hand on the small of my back as we head toward the cabin. When we reach the steps, Kole hangs back, looking around as if he's checking that no one has followed us—even though we know no one could breach the mask. The others file past, up toward the veranda, but I choose to hang back with Kole.

Sam glances at me but I flick my eyes to the door, hoping he understands that I'll catch up in a minute.

Realizing we're alone, Kole tries to move past me but— standing a few steps higher than him so our eyes are level—I catch his arm. "Whatever you can't tell me, it's okay."

He's barely moving, barely even breathing. I stroke his face. "It's okay, my gorgeous Viking. It's okay."

Closing his eyes, for just a moment, he leans into my touch. When he looks at me again, his words drip through me like raindrops. *I love you, Nova.*

The words themselves don't surprise me, but the force with which they enter my body does. I lean in, expecting him to kiss me. Before he can, Tanner appears at the door. "You two alright?" he asks.

"Good." Kole nods at me, then lets go of my waist and nudges past to stride up the steps.

As he disappears inside, Tanner raises his eyebrows at me.

"He's not okay," I tell him.

Tanner sits down on the top step. "I know."

I sit beside him and shake my head. "He knows something he can't share with us."

Again, Tanner says, "I know."

"That's a heavy weight to carry."

"It is." Tanner is staring out at the lake. I inch closer and run my palm over his back. His muscles are taut beneath my hand. I rub his neck a little and he closes his eyes. Giving me a dimpled smile, he says, "I haven't seen nearly enough of you the past few days."

"You've been with me the entire time," I tease, nudging him with my elbow.

"But I haven't been *with* you since the train." Tanner suddenly flips himself over and, as if he's doing some kind of fancy press-up, positions himself in front of me. His hands are on either side of my legs, his feet balanced precariously on a lower step. "I meant what I said about that dress." He wiggles his eyebrows at me. "Don't suppose you brought it back with you?"

"'Fraid not." I laugh and use my knees to pull him farther up my body. I arch back uncomfortably, trapped between Tanner's heavy chest and the wooden step behind my back.

"When all of this is over, remind me to take you shopping again." He plants a row of kisses down my jawline, the contact with his warm mouth making me sigh.

But then a heaviness settles inside me. "Will it be over?" I ask. "Will there be an *afterwards* or is this it? Can we actually do this, Tanner? Can we win against Ragnor?" I can't bring myself to say any more. Nico might be able to speak the devil's name, but it burns like hot coals in my mouth.

Tanner stiffens against me, but not in an erotic way. When he meets my eyes, his shoulders drop and he moves back to where he was before, sitting next to me instead of on top of me. "The prophecy says we can." He cocks his head in my direction. "We have to believe that."

I nod slowly. I want to believe it. Before we visited Kole's commune, I did believe it. But after the vision that caused Kole to black out, and whatever else he saw that he can't share with us, I'm not so certain anymore. I'm not so certain that my destiny is to triumph over evil.

What if my destiny is to lose?

SAM

The others are washing up—a strangely normal activity considering what we've just been through —when I see Nova and Luther at the end of the jetty. They disappeared sometime after we finished eating, and curiosity made me follow.

He's holding out his hands. Flames are in them. She tips her head back as he traces her silhouette with his fire barely a whisker away from her pale skin.

A knot tightens in my chest. Darkness clouds my vision. Sprinting down the steps, I hurtle toward them and grab him by the shoulders. He's bigger than me, but I can take him.

When I throw him to the ground, he looks up, startled, but doesn't fight back.

Nova tugs my arm. "Sam? What are you doing?"

I'm shaking. I've been in the fire playroom in *Spine* enough times to know what some fire mages find sexy. Scarred flesh. The smell of burning. "Are you alright?" I pull her in front of me, examine her arms, study her face.

"I'm fine," she says, easing away from me and helping Luther up from the floor. "We were just… playing."

"It's dangerous." I fix my eyes on hers. "He could hurt you —even if he doesn't mean to."

"He can't hurt me." Nova shakes her head. "It's hard to explain."

"Show him." Luther is behind Nova, scowling at me. He blinks the flames back into his hands, and she closes her eyes as he begins to move them close to her. It takes every ounce of willpower inside me not to wrench her away from him, but then I realize what's happening; the flames don't touch her. As if an invisible forcefield surrounds her, they curve backward, away from her skin.

Luther clenches his fists, and the fire disappears.

"I still don't like it," I tell her.

"Then don't watch." Luther cocks an eyebrow at me, but Nova moves between us.

"I don't want him to watch," she says softly, staring up into Luther's face.

Luther's lips twitch into a smile, then he looks me up and down. "Whatever you say, Little Star. Just tell us where you want us."

Nova bites her lower lip for a moment, studying the two of us as though she's genuinely running through different scenarios in her head.

"Undress me," she says, positioning herself between us.

Luther doesn't hesitate, he pulls her sweater up over her head then crouches down and peels her jeans over her voluptuous thighs.

Behind her, still fizzing with annoyance at Luther, I try to focus only on Nova, which is hard because his hands are all over her and watching his mouth land on her stomach makes my dick twitch uncomfortably.

While he swirls his fierce tongue past her belly button and up over her sides, I unhook her bra and replace it with my hands, holding her breasts, rubbing my thumbs over her nipples.

Instantly, I'm hard. Noticing, she presses her ass against my groin. Then she sinks to her knees and gives Luther's jeans a little tug. He kneels in front of her, and she fumbles with his buttons. When they're open, as she nips his lower lip with her teeth, she rubs the palm of her hand over the imprint of his erection. It's still hidden inside his black boxers, so I wait with anticipation for her to tug it free.

When she does, I lower myself to the ground and look over her shoulder. He's pierced—a ladder of metal bars decorates his shaft, and two round silver balls protrude from the head. Fuck, that must have hurt. By the stars, it looks good though.

Nova sits back and admires him. She traces her fingers over the bars, fascinated.

Luther watches her with a mixture of pride and lust on his face, then he puts his hands on her sides and encourages her to bend over onto all fours.

When she does, presenting her ass to me, I smooth my palms over her cheeks. As I drag my finger over the cleft of her ass, between her cheeks to her pussy, she wriggles back a little and opens her legs for me.

Jerking my sweatpants down over my hips, I pull my cock free and position myself at her entrance. As I ease into her cunt, she starts to swirl her tongue around the swollen head of Luther's pierced dick. She flicks the piercings, laps at them, then follows the ladder up and down. She takes him deep into her mouth but doesn't gag. With her hand, she massages the part of his shaft that hasn't passed her lips. He grabs her shoulders and thrusts into her. This time, she does gag.

"Fuck, Nova, you look so good swallowing my metal." Luther winds his fingers into her hair.

Watching him fuck her mouth, I'm ready to explode. She's heating up on the inside, clenching tight around me, and I'll be done in seconds if this carries on.

Reaching around, I find her clit and start to massage it. Taking her mouth from Luther's cock, she braces her hands on the ground so I can fuck her harder. I curl over her body, pressing her top half down into the ground as I lift up on one knee and thrust deeper into her pussy. Watching us with fire in his eyes, Luther holds her still for me.

The sound of my balls slapping against her makes stars appear in front of my eyes. "Nova, I'm going to come. I'm sorry I—"

She doesn't reply, just purposefully slams back onto my shaft.

When I come, it's quick and violent. My body shakes, I fall forward and bite her shoulder. Not hard enough to draw blood like Kole, just enough to send a vibration of pleasure up through my jaw.

I've barely finished leaking into her cunt when Luther picks her up and turns her over. Lying on her back, she rests her head on my knees and holds my hands while Luther palms himself into oblivion. When he shoots hot jets of cum onto her chest, he tips his head back and sighs. His shoulders drop. Every ounce of tension leaves his body.

Together, we massage his milky liquid into her skin while she closes her eyes and hums softly.

As our orgasms subside, we lie side-by-side on the jetty. Nova rests her head on my chest. Luther curls behind her.

The three of us stay like that for a long time, kissing her and touching her. Not because we want to have sex again, but to remind ourselves she's here and that she's ours.

After a while, kissing Nova on the head, Luther gives a loud yawn. "I'll see you in bed," he says—surprisingly softly—

staggering to his feet. "Don't stay out too late. It's getting cold."

When he's gone, I move over to the mooring at the side of the jetty and lean against it. Nova nestles into me. The blanket that lies in a crumpled heap on the ground tells me she and Luther had been planning to be out here a while. I pick it up and wrap it around us as she settles between my legs, resting her back against my chest.

We sit in silence, staring out at the darkening sky. A breeze drifts across the lake, carrying the scent of pine trees and night.

Eventually, Nova whispers, "Do you want to talk about it?" She turns in my lap and trails a knowing hand over the scarred planes of my chest, her fingers skimming the soft silvery-purple rivets. "The reason you freaked out with Luther back there?"

I close my eyes, pulling the blanket close around her chest. I want to tell her; I want her to know the darkest depths of my soul. But at the same time, they feel too distant to matter. Far away. Like they happened to another person in another life.

Wrapping my arms tight around her waist, leaning on the tall wooden mooring at the end of the jetty, I kiss the soft spot between her neck and her shoulder. "After Alice and Charles died, and the doctors told me you..." I can't say the words. Nova strokes my arms and lifts my hand to kiss my knuckles. "I was sent to a kids' home, then foster care."

"Me too," Nova whispers.

"Pretty much all of them were shitty."

"Mine too," she says, lacing her fingers with mine.

"The last was the worst. They were in debt up to their eyeballs. So, they decided to sell me."

Nova stiffens in my arms. "They sold you?"

"To Madame." I tug Nova a little closer, centering myself

with her warmth. "For a while, it actually wasn't too bad. At the club I had food and a roof over my head. No friends— they didn't like us socializing—but we had movie night once a week." I shake my head, sadness swishing in my stomach as I think of how grateful sixteen-year-old Sam was just to have a bed to sleep in and food in his belly. "Madame must have seen something in me. I don't know what. She decided to let me stay a..." I shift uncomfortably.

"A virgin?" Nova asks, staring out at the darkening lake.

I rest my chin on the top of her head. "I didn't have to do the same stuff the others did. I was lucky. I just danced. For a long time, I just danced."

"When did the..." Nova searches for the word. "When did they start using you for the...?"

"The wolf dances?" I stroke a small scar on the top of her arm, then walk my fingers across her chest. "When I turned twenty." Catching her face and turning it to mine, I kiss her softly. "You saved me," I whisper. "I'd heard them talking about selling me in an auction. For my virginity."

Nova presses her forehead to mine. She moves her lips to my neck then down to my collar bone, her tongue tracing the contours of my past. Then she shifts so she's sitting sideways on my lap, her warm naked body pressed up against me, arms looped around my neck. I part her folds with my fingers and take my time exploring her pussy. She moans quietly as I try to memorize the feel of her. She is warm and wet and takes my finger with ease. I slide in another, then another, pressing my palm to her core as I fuck her languidly with my fingers.

"Sam..." She reaches for my erection, but I stop her.

"No, just you," I mutter. "I want to see my supernova spark."

She starts to rock forward onto my fingers, clinging onto my neck as she hovers on the edge of her orgasm. When she comes, it is slow and shuddering. Her body melts into my arms. She sighs and quivers as she presses herself against me.

I'm used to feeling unsatisfied. More times than I can count, I've watched strangers fucking in the darkness and had to swallow down my own arousal. Ignore it. Dampen it. I've already come once this evening; I don't deserve more than that.

I hug Nova close, expecting her to fall asleep in my arms. Instead, she pivots, straddles me, and slides onto my aching shaft. Having her like this is a new kind of pleasure. With her back pressed to my chest, my hands are able to cup her breasts, travel over her stomach, play with her clit. Moving away from the mooring, I lay flat on my back, expecting her to turn around so she's facing me. Instead, she braces her hands on my thighs and folds herself over, giving me a mouth-watering view of my cock moving in and out of her cunt.

I spread her cheeks and groan loudly as I thrust up into her. Reaching between my legs, she starts to play with my balls, and strokes the velvety skin behind them. My eyes roll back in my head. I grab her hips, pinch her gorgeously soft skin between my fingers, then release my thick, hot liquid inside her for the second time tonight.

When she stands, the cold is unbearable. Reaching for my hand, she tugs me to my feet. I grab the blanket and wrap it around her shoulders, then pick up our clothes. "I think we need a hot shower," she says, kissing my chest.

"I think you're right."

* * *

AFTER OUR SHOWER, we climb into bed with the others. I position myself on the edge. Now Luther's here too, it's a tight squeeze. I wait until Nova's breathing changes, and her face becomes smooth with the peace of sleep. Then I unfold myself from the mattress, pick up my clothes, and head downstairs.

In the darkness of the living room, I tug on my sweatpants, t-shirt, and a navy sweater I borrowed from Tanner. I take one last look around the cabin, at the remnants of the strange life we've shared here, then I walk out of the door.

I'm standing at the foot of the steps, ready to shift and become the wolf version of myself, when I hear footsteps behind me. I turn to find Kole and Tanner staring down at me from the veranda.

"Midnight run?" Kole asks darkly.

Tanner takes the steps quickly and comes to a stop in front of me. "You're leaving?" he asks, searching my face. "Where are you going?"

"To The Hollow." I put my hands into my pockets.

"For Nico?" Tanner's face contorts into a frown.

"For Nova," I reply. "They'll let me in. Ragnor has no idea I've met the five of you. If I tell him I've tracked him down, he'll let me in. I can help cause a distraction and give you a chance."

"Have you spoken to Nova?" Kole appears at Tanner's side.

I shake my head. "She'd say no."

A trembling silence hangs in the air.

"I have to do this, Tanner." I meet his eyes. "I left her alone. For years, something in my gut told me she was out there, and I ignored it. I didn't try to find her. I didn't protect her. But she found me, and she saved me, and now it's my turn to try and save her."

Tanner's about to speak when Kole puts a heavy hand on my shoulder and says, "Good luck, brother."

Tears bite at my throat. I pat Kole's hand. "Thank you, brother."

"You're okay with this?" Tanner looks at Kole. "You think this is a good idea?"

Kole presses his lips together, then suddenly I get it; he knows this has to happen. He's seen something. Whatever his vision showed him in the forest, and whatever he said to his mother in private, he knows I have to leave.

Somehow, knowing my decision is something to do with fate makes me feel braver.

Tanner pulls me into a fierce embrace. "Take care of yourself," he says. "If she loses you again, it'll break her."

"I will." I stand back and grip his upper arms. "I'll get past the barrier and do my best to distract them when the time comes." I laugh a little and shake my head. As I walk away from them, I call back, "Might even get close enough to kill Ragnor myself."

37

TANNER

When Sam's wolfish tail disappears into the trees, I round on Kole. "What did you see?" I stare up into his face. I'm not short, but his six-foot five frame towers over my five-eleven physique. "Kole, what did you see?"

Kole's eyes swim with darkness. He's come down from the blood rush he got on the train, but something else simmers there. "I can't tell you, Tanner."

"Fuck that!" I hiss, pushing my chest against his. "She can't lose him again, so if he's about to go get himself killed, we have to stop him."

Kole shakes his head. "We can't." As I clench my jaw and stride away from him, Kole catches my arm. "You know I can't reveal—"

"You did for me. When you saw me. Trapped. Tortured." I tug my arm back. "You told the others what you saw, and you came to rescue me. You pulled me out of hell, Kole. *You* did that."

"Because the vision showed me that I had to." He sighs,

frustration creasing his features. We've never fought like this before, especially about visions and prophecies and how fucking complicated that shit gets. I know I'm being an asshole. "You're scared for her," Kole says, meeting my eyes. "I am, too."

I press my lips together.

"But she'll be okay. Sam has to go, and we have to stay, and that's the way it has to be." He nods at me, rising up to his full height and folding his arms in front of his chest.

Instead of softening and being friends again, I push past him and mutter, "I'm not telling her. You can tell her, but I'm not."

* * *

WHILE KOLE CLIMBS BACK into bed with Nova, I pace the living room. At some point just before dawn, Luther appears. "You look like hell," he says. "What's going on?"

I'm about to tell him when the sound of Nova shouting makes us both look up toward the ceiling. A moment later, as Luther lurches toward the other side of the room, Nova thunders down the stairs. She trips at the bottom, falls to the floor, scrambles to her feet, then hurtles toward the door. She's barely outside when she starts shouting Sam's name.

"What the fuck?" Luther shoots me a quizzical stare before charging after her.

I linger for a moment. Pure, unadulterated panic swells in the room. Panic and fear. I push my fingers through my hair, trying to block out the sound of Nova starting to cry as she tells Luther what's happened.

When Kole and Mack emerge from the bedroom, Kole's expression is unreadable. Mack, however, looks like he's ready to play peacekeeper. "Kole told me," he says when he reaches me. "You okay?"

"I am. She's not." I gesture to the door.

Mack's about to go out there when it swings back on its hinges and Luther strides in with Nova slung over his shoulder. If she wasn't genuinely upset, it would be kind of a turn on because she's pummeling his back and her ass is sticking up in the air.

He deposits her on the couch. "Nova, breathe." He crouches in front of her and rubs her knees. "Breathe."

Wiping her face, Nova searches for me. Her anger has softened and now all that radiates from her face is hurt. "Why didn't you stop him?" she asks in a voice that makes my stomach curl.

"He'd made up his mind, Nova. He wanted to do it." I leverage myself over the back of the couch and land heavily next to her. "He'll be okay." I meet her eyes. "He'll be fine. All he's going to do is cause a distraction, so we can try and bring down the barrier."

"That's all?" She looks past me, directing her question to Kole.

If he knows more than that, he doesn't let it show in his face. He simply nods and says, "That's all."

"You'd tell me if there was more?" She stands, staring at him. We all stare at him.

"I'd tell you if there was more." The lie rolls easily off Kole's tongue. He can't tell Nova the truth; if he told her some ancient laws prevent seers from revealing more than snippets of their visions, she simply wouldn't understand. Heck, I gave him a hard enough time for it last night and I've grown up knowing this stuff.

He wouldn't tell her if there was more unless the vision made it clear he *should* tell her. But exposing him now, in front of her, won't do anything useful.

Right now, she needs us united, and we need to focus.

Because we have less than twenty-four hours to stop what's about to happen.

To stop the next domino falling.

To stop The Shadow King having Nova's name on his lips.

38

NICO

The Hollow is quiet. Deathly quiet. I slip through the dark corridors, past the bedrooms that—less than a few weeks ago—belonged to Nova and the others. Ragnor doesn't seem to sleep. He's set up residence in the lounge. The room with the swanky pop-up bathtub and the large fireplace. From there, he can see out to the lawn. From there, he can watch Eve as she continues her never-ending preparation work for the ritual.

I have no idea what the ritual itself involves. Mother doesn't seem to, either. Only that it has to happen when the moon is full. Yesterday, Eve had Andre catch six rabbits. She skinned them and drained their blood, which now sits decanted into several glass vials on top of the altar she's constructed in the garden.

She has skulls too. Black feathers. Herbs and crystals. All of which she is continually rearranging while chattering to herself under her breath. She's barely eaten since we got here. In fact, the only thing I've seen her consume is large quantities of F.H.B.

Ragnor doesn't seem to care; the only thing he cares about is Elena.

While everyone else sleeps, I head for the kitchen, make coffee, and go to sit on the concrete steps that lead down to the fountain. For perhaps the first time in days, Eve isn't here. Elena's coffin is closed, lying in front of the altar. Eve's strange collection of objects surrounds it.

I'm tempted to go down there and steal something—a feather, a skull, a bag of strange-looking herbs—just to see if it would make any different. But what I told Nova and the others was true; I'm a fucking coward. Even the thought of it makes me feel sick to my stomach.

When I returned from their cabin in the woods, I couldn't quite believe I'd had the nerve to go through with my plan to help them. I felt sure that my mother would know what I'd done as soon as she saw me, or that Ragnor would have had me followed, or that I'd give the game away myself by being so hell-damned pathetic.

But they didn't suspect anything. Barely even noticed I'd been gone for a few hours.

I look at my phone for the time. I should have given Nova my cell number. At least then she might have been able to contact me and tell me what was happening. But who am I kidding? Like she'd have trusted me enough to tell me anything.

I don't blame her. How could she possibly trust me after what I did? After the lies I told?

I'm ignoring the sting of hot coffee in my mouth when a familiar scent drifts toward me on the breeze. I put the cup down so quickly that liquid sloshes over the rim and stains the concrete below it. "Sam?"

I bolt for the trees, following the scent. As I draw closer, I know I'm not mistaken.

When I reach the barrier, my brother is staring at me

from the other side of it. He raises his hand, palm-out, a cross between a wave and a salute.

"What are you doing here?" I ask, panic flushing my cheeks. "Are the others with you?"

Sam shakes his head. "I came to…" He pauses. "Can you let me in?"

Hissing, my heart beating so hard I feel like I might crack a rib, I reply, "Sam, you can't come in here. It's too dangerous."

"I'm here for Nova," Sam says, his eyes widening. "So I can create a distraction while they try to get past the barrier."

I'm surprised he's giving me this much information. He knows nothing about me, except what Nova must have told him. Yet, I can see it in his face—he trusts me.

"It's too dangerous—"

"Nico, please. One of us has to do it." He fixes his eyes on mine. Shame hums in my chest. He knows it won't be me. "What will you tell Ragnor?"

"I'll tell him I tracked him down. That the adoption agency told me his name and I did a tracking spell to find him."

"That won't work." I shake my head. "He's got defenses against spells like that." My mind moves quickly. "Andre, one of Ragnor's wolves, has a cousin. A deadbeat who hangs out on the F.H.B circuit. He's the runner who brings Eve's supply up here."

"Does this guy ever work *Spine*?" Sam asks.

"What dealers *don't* frequent *Spine*?" I ask, frowning.

"Good. That works." Sam folds his arms. Without a hint of self-pity, he says, "I worked in *Spine* from the age of sixteen. So, that story makes sense—Sarah could have given me Ragnor's name, and I could have tracked him down via Eve's contact."

"Sarah?" I don't know that name.

"The woman who—" Sam shakes his head. "It doesn't matter. What's the cousin called?"

"Don't know. Don't think it matters." I glance back at the house then at Sam again. "You're sure about this?"

He barely moves as he replies, "Yes, I'm sure."

"Okay, well I can't just let you in. I'll have to go raise the alarm." I swipe my fingers through my hair. Nerves, like a thousand needles, prickle my skin. "I'll try to look out for you but remember we've never met. I'm not even supposed to know you exist. If Ragnor knew my mother had told me about you—"

"I won't say anything that would get you in trouble, Nico." Sam's voice is surprisingly warm. Kind. As if he truly wouldn't want something bad to happen to me.

Before returning to the house, I pause. "I hope this isn't the last time we get to speak to one another," I tell him.

Sam meets my eyes as I look back over my shoulder and says, "I hope so too."

* * *

INSIDE, I stop in the entrance hall. It's large with a gray flagstone floor and a sweeping staircase that leads to the upstairs of the house. I approach the door to the lounge. My palms are sweating. My father has always made me nervous, but now—as ashamed as I am to admit it—I'm terrified of him.

I've always seen disappointment in his eyes but, since I failed and ran away from my undercover mission at The Hollow, I now see something else too. Disgust.

I knock hesitantly. When there's no answer, I draw in a deep breath and knock louder. Still no answer, I push the door open to find my father standing completely naked in front of the fire. His hands are braced on the mantle, bulky shoulders rippling. Eve is kneeling in front of him.

Shoving her away from him, he whirls around, eyes flashing with anger as he yanks his pants back up.

Eve wipes her mouth and stands. Her eyes are completely black. Pools of liquid ink. She smiles at me and saunters over.

"What the fuck do you want, Nico?" Ragnor spits.

"I think he wants to join us," Eve coos, running her thin fingers up my chest.

"Eve," Ragnor growls.

"There's something you need to see." I speak up before either of them can say anything else. "Outside. Someone who says he's your son." I fix my eyes on Ragnor's. I study his face.

His expression doesn't change. Is he so utterly devoid of feeling that he doesn't give a damn the son he abandoned twenty years ago is now on his doorstep? Heck, even curious about how he found us here?

Wordlessly, Ragnor pushes past me. He doesn't bother putting on a shirt, just strides through the house with me at his heels. "Where?" he snaps.

"Outside."

Once we get outside, he stops in front of the fountain, glaring at me. "Show me."

Eve is skipping behind us, her dress caught in her panties, exposing a flash of her milky white thigh. "Another son? Ragnor, how lucky. Now I'll have three boys to play with."

Again, my father ignores her.

I lead him down toward the barrier. While half of me is desperate to see Sam again, the other half prays he'll have changed his mind and run back to Nova. But no. He's right where I left him.

Taking in Ragnor's form, Sam draws himself up to his full height and simply glowers at him. Fuck, I wish I could be that brave in our father's presence.

"Sam?" Ragnor's eyes twitch. He trails his gaze up and down Sam's body. "You've grown."

"That happens over the course of twenty years," Sam replies in a steady tone.

"How did you find me?" Ragnor folds his arms.

"Contacts," Sam replies.

My chest tightens. Don't be too cocky, Sam. Please, don't be too cocky.

Ragnor's jaw twitches. "What do you want?"

"I want to talk."

"Now isn't a good time," Ragnor replies without a hint of irony.

"I can wait." Sam's stance is rigid, making it clear he is not going to leave any time soon.

Nostrils flaring, Ragnor is silent for a moment then flicks his eyes toward Eve. "Let him in," he spits.

Clapping with glee, Eve reaches out, her arm crackling like static as she pushes it through the barrier. Taking hold of Sam, she tugs him onto our side. It makes his hair stand on end, and he combs his fingers through to smooth it.

"This way," Ragnor barks.

Sam follows him. Taking in the state of the lawn, his eyes catch on the coffin. I watch him swallow, his Adam's apple bobbing up and down. He clenches his fists at his sides but forces himself to look away from it.

Inside, Ragnor takes us back through the house. In the lounge, he tells Sam to sit down but Sam shakes his head. "No thanks," he says, positioning himself by the window.

This time, Ragnor does reach for a shirt. Shrugging himself into it, he looks at Eve. "Fetch Kayla and tell Andre to bring us some coffee." When Eve disappears, he sits down on the couch and rests his forearms on his thighs. "Well, Sam," he says. "As you're here, I suppose I should introduce you to your brother."

39

SAM

On the outside I'm calm but my insides are a mess. I'm doing a better job of holding it together than Nico, though, because he looks like he's about to puke all over the fancy rug.

He does an okay job of seeming shocked when Ragnor tells him I'm his brother, muttering, "Elena had a son?" with enough conviction that Ragnor jerks him up from his chair and grabs him by the collar.

"You don't speak her name, do you understand?" he spits.

Nico nods, his hands shaking.

Watching their interaction, it takes a lot not to dive in and stick up for Nico. Being here, seeing it first-hand, it's painfully obvious he's been manipulated by Ragnor his entire life. Working in *Spine* did a lot of things to me, but at least it didn't make me feel worthless. In a strange way, I felt valued. My body, what I did, they were important.

Nico, however, has been made to believe he has nothing of value to offer anyone. Nova told me he's famous. When she said the name—Nico Varlac—it rang a bell. I think he visited the club once or twice, although I hope he didn't ever frequent the wolf dance because that would be too fucking creepy.

He doesn't seem like a famous person here, though. He seems like a scared kid. A kid who's desperate for his father's approval and has finally realized he's not ever going to get it.

Nico is nodding, still in Ragnor's grasp, when the door clatters open. A tall, short-haired woman strides in. She's very clearly Nico's mother. Kayla? Was that her name?

Tugging him away from our father, Kayla doesn't seem concerned or upset. She doesn't check him over or ask if he's okay, but she does stare daggers at Ragnor. It takes her a moment to register I'm in the room. When she sees me, her eyes widen. She looks at Nico and claps a hand over her mouth.

"They look so alike, don't they?" The witch—who must be the one called Eve—stands between us. A grin stretches her thin lips. "How lovely for them to be reunited at a time like this."

"How did you find me?" Ragnor cuts in, repeating the question I still haven't answered.

"You remember a woman called Sarah?" I don't look away from Ragnor's face.

"I remember her," he replies.

"She tracked me down. Told me your name."

"That doesn't explain how you found us here," Kayla interjects. She's got a nasty scar on her face. Jagged and purple.

"When Sarah found me, I was working at a club in Red Rock. I asked around about you." I jerk my head to Ragnor. "A wolf F.H.B dealer said you'd cleared out after a fire at your hotel. Said he could tell me where you were if I could pay."

Ragnor's eyes snap toward Eve. "I told you not to let that weasel come here," he spits.

Eve doesn't apologize, just shrugs and says, "If I hadn't,

they wouldn't have found each other. It's perfect." She hums and hugs her waist. "Utterly perfect." She moves closer to me and runs her hand up my arm. "He'll be here to greet his mother when she returns."

Nausea bites at my throat. Pretending I don't know what the hell Eve's talking about, I say, "My mother is dead."

"Yes," Ragnor replies. "She is, but not for much longer."

* * *

OUR STRANGE, tense reunion continues for a few more minutes before Ragnor tells me that now that I'm here I'll have to stay until 'the ritual' is done. He doesn't seem to care that he hasn't explained what the ritual is or that we've been reunited after twenty years apart. He also doesn't give a shit that Nico, as far as he knows, just found out he has a half-brother.

"We begin at midnight. I want you all there." Ragnor scowls at Kayla, then gestures to the door.

As we file toward it, I try to muster something close to annoyance and turn back to him. "That's it? I can stay and watch your freaky ritual, whatever the fuck that's about, but you don't have time to speak to me? You can't give me more than five minutes after *twenty years*? Do you know what happened to me? Do you know where I ended up? Do you care?"

Waiting for his reply, I'm not sure whether what I just said came from a place of truth or if it's an act.

Before Ragnor can reply, Eve wraps her fingers around my wrist. She squeezes hard, nails dig into my flesh. "You shouldn't speak to your father that way," she hisses. "Not when he's—"

"Eve. Stop." Ragnor steps in. His eyes flicker with something gray and ice-cold. "Let's leave it as a surprise, shall we?"

It takes a few seconds for Eve to let go of me. When she does, she speaks through gritted teeth, "Fine. As you say, Master."

When the study door closes, Eve blows Kayla a kiss and trots back in the direction of the garden. Kayla's face is pale. Tugging Nico toward the front door, she heaves it open and shoves him outside. I follow them.

When it has closed behind us, she puts her hands on his shoulders and barks, "What is this? What did you do, Nico? Did you bring him here?"

"How could I?" Nico stutters, wincing under his mother's grip.

She blinks at him, then looks at me.

"I didn't know he existed until about ten minutes ago," I tell her. "I came here looking for my father. I had no idea I had a brother."

"He's not your brother," Kayla spits, rounding on me. "He's nothing to you. Do you understand?"

"Mom…" Nico tugs her arm gently. "It's okay. I'd like to…" He pauses, chewing the inside of his lip. "I'd like to get to know him. I always wanted a brother—"

With an exasperated eye roll, Kayla turns back to the door. Her hand is on the doorknob when she says, "Fine, play happy families for tonight, but don't get attached. Ragnor won't want him around once—" She stops and looks at me over her shoulder. From her expression, it's obvious she wants to tell me what Ragnor's planning. That she wants to be the one to tell me he's going to bring my mother back to life, just so she can see the hurt and confusion in my face. But she must be scared of him too, because she says nothing.

When she's gone, and we're alone, Nico nods toward the steps. "If we head round this way, we'll reach the kitchen," he says. "Andre never did appear with that coffee."

As we walk side-by-side, I look up at the house. It's huge

and imposing and cloaked the kind of darkness that seeps into your bones. Not literal darkness—a darkness that threatens to eat at your soul if you let it in.

"So, it's happening tonight?" I ask quietly. "Do you know how?"

Nico shakes his head. We've rounded the corner of the building. In front of us, I see the fountain and the back of Eve's altar. My mother's coffin is obscured from view. "I guess it involves that stuff," he says, pointing to the two long rows of skulls that form a kind of aisle in front of the coffin. "But she's been rearranging it for days. Not sure she even knows what she's doing." A little hopefully, he says, "Maybe it won't work. Maybe she's not as powerful as Ragnor thinks."

Reaching the steps that lead up to the kitchen, Nico leads the way. The room is a mess. Windows blown in, broken glass underfoot, dirty dishes piled high in the sink.

Nico ignores it all and puts the kettle on the stove. As I lean back against the counter, he does the same opposite me. We don't speak until the kettle has boiled and he's made a fresh pot of coffee. Pouring us each a mug, he gestures back to the garden. We're on the lawn when he says, "We need to stay where they can see us, but preferably far enough out of the way that they can't hear us."

I nod, even though I wish we could have found somewhere without a view of my dead mother's coffin.

"Where have you been?" Nico asks, holding his mug close to his lips. "What happened after I left?"

I hesitate, unsure how much I should tell him. At this point, I don't suppose anything I tell him will matter much; it's not as if we have a grand plan that could be foiled if Ragnor knew about it. Our only plan is to walk up and hope Nova's powers kick in enough to stop what's about to happen. "We went to visit the seer who was first sent the prophecy."

Nico watches me intently. "Did they help you?"

"She showed us *why* we're involved in the prophecy. Us and Nova. But I'm not sure how it helps."

Nico stares down into his coffee. When he takes a sip, he winces. "Usually take sugar, but we're out," he says.

"Me too," I reply, my eyes landing on the birthmark on Nico's wrist.

"I really have always wanted a brother," he says.

"Were you lonely growing up?" I ask as we walk slowly across the lawn.

"I'm still lonely." Nico meets my eyes. Something in his face makes my stomach twist with sympathy.

"Hey," I say, trying to lighten the mood even though I'm pretty sure that's impossible when you're facing death at any moment. "Until a week ago, I lived in a cage underneath a nightclub. I know a bit about loneliness."

"You lived at that place?" Nico asks. "*Spine?*"

I nod. I'm not really ready to tell him the full story, but a nagging feeling in my gut tells me we might not get another chance. The next few hours could be the only hours I have with my brother. If things don't go our way, they could be the only hours most of us have before hell breaks loose and The Shadow King destroys humanity. So, I suck in a deep breath and I start from the beginning. "I remember living with Ragnor in a big house. Sarah looked after me. I was three, I think. Then he gave me up..."

As I speak, Nico listens. He listens to the whole, sorry story of my life. And then he tells me his. By the time we're done, I feel more at peace than I have in a long time, and I think he does too, because he says, "Thank you, Sam," and puts his arm around me. "Thanks for trusting me."

"Don't make me regret it," I tell him.

"I won't," he says. "I promise you, I won't."

NOVA

We leave the cabin at eleven p.m. and take the truck we borrowed from Kole's contact in the valley. Before we reach the winding road that leads to The Hollow, we park.

It takes about thirty minutes for us to walk the rest of the way, branching off into the wood well before reaching The Hollow's gates.

As we walk, my blood grows colder. It's been a long time since I felt chilled on the inside, but Kole and Tanner were right; there is evil here. A darkness that makes me feel like there will be no tomorrow. No light. Endless nothingness with no reprieve.

My footsteps seem to whisper *Sam, Sam, Sam* as they pound the damp earth. I can't believe he left, and I can't believe he didn't at least say goodbye to me. Fear pulls my heart taut in my chest. It feels like it might tear at any moment, and the thought of never seeing his face again after only just getting him back is too much to bear.

When Tanner looks at me, I'm crying. Big, silent tears roll

down my cheeks. He pulls me into his arms and stops to hold me for a moment.

"Nova," he says, "try to stay strong. We need to focus."

On the other side of me, Mack adds, "Use what you're feeling. Remember what we saw." He places a firm hand on my stomach. "Use it to channel your magick."

I tell him I will, but I'm not sure I believe it; how can I channel power, and fire, and fury when all I feel is a near-paralyzing terror?

Eve's barrier is like the one Mack and Luther set up at The Hollow before the Bureau agents came for us. Standing in the shadow of the trees, we can see the mansion in front of us. The lawn. The fountain.

Memories dance in front of my eyes, but they're torn away when I notice the altar. Constructed so it's opposite the fountain, a coffin is in front of it. Two lines of skulls form an eerie walkway. On top of the altar, more strange objects, and a large leather-bound book.

"What do we do?" I ask Kole.

He doesn't answer me.

"Wait until they come outside. Sam told Kole and Tanner he'd cause a distraction, so we look for his cue, then break down the barrier." Mack looks up, examining the shield in front of us.

"How?" I ask.

"Like when we put up the mask at the cabin, we'll join hands and combine our forces." He fixes his eyes on mine as he mutters an incantation that I struggle to remember. "The spell will weaken it, then it'll be a matter of brute force to get through."

I blink at him. "Right. Spell then force. Got it."

Mack's about to say something else when movement catches my eyes. Up ahead, a tall blond-haired man has appeared. Kayla is on one side. Eve is on the other. They file quietly down the steps until Eve breaks ranks and skips the rest of the way to the altar. When Ragnor and Kayla are positioned in front of it, looking out toward the fountain, more people appear.

Werewolves, some of whom I recognize from the hotel, jostle each other as they move to stand in whispering clusters on either side of the aisle of skulls.

Finally, I see Sam. He and Nico appear together and walk side-by-side down the steps. Sam glances in our direction. I have no idea if he can smell us. No one else seems to, but perhaps he's more in tune with my scent than they are.

Ragnor indicates that Nico and Sam should stand at the very front of the crowd to the right of the altar.

When everyone is in position, Eve starts talking. It's a tongue I don't understand. Next to me, Mack whispers, "*Mageia*," but he doesn't interpret.

She waves her arms at the sky, then waves Ragnor forward. He lowers himself toward the coffin and heaves off its lid. My breath catches in my throat, but as he leans down over it—like he's about to lift out a delicate porcelain doll—a howl ripples the air.

Sam has shifted. He lurches for Ragnor, clamps his teeth on his forearm, and clamps down. Ragnor yells and tries to throw him off, but Sam's jaw is like a vice. Chaos breaks out. Other wolves shift and lunge for Sam. Ragnor shifts too, but Sam keeps hold of him.

"Now," Mack whispers. Peeling my eyes away from Sam, I join hands with him. We form a circle and start to chant.

Beyond the barrier, all I hear is teeth and growls and yelps. They remind me of *Spine*. The stage. Sam's hypnotic dance. Anger billows inside me. It rushes up my spine like lava from a volcano and explodes. I roar and tip my head back.

Mack lets go of my hand. I vaguely sense that I burned

him, but it's as if I'm not really here. I'm not Nova. I am fire, and heat, and fury.

As the barrier drops, the earth starts to shake, and I have no idea if I'm causing it or if it was Eve.

The earth rumbles beneath my feet. Vibrations spike up through my soles. There's a cracking sound, then another, and then the ground splits open.

Luther pulls me to the side, throwing his body on top of mine. Mack and Tanner are opposite us, stumbling back as the crack widens and thick black smoke billows up from it. Next to me, Kole splays his fingers and directs his palms toward the ground as he tries to sew it back together with the roots underneath. The crack starts to close, but then he's flung backward, and it continues to grow.

Luther and I haul Kole to his feet. Mack meets my eyes and shouts, "This way, run!" hurtling toward The Hollow.

Opposite the fountain, Ragnor's wolves are baying at the moon. Sam is on the ground, being pinned down by three of Ragnor's henchmen. Eve stretches her arms wide as lightning almost splits the sky open. She is chanting at the top of her voice. Without looking at us, she sweeps her hand in our direction and—just like the last time she captured me—I'm helpless.

In unison, we are thrown to our knees. I struggle against the restraints but it's futile.

"Fuck!" Luther yells. "Fuck!"

"It's no use," Kole growls. "She's too strong."

I try to lock eyes on Sam again. He's human now, still on the ground with wolves at his sides. Next to him, Nico stares wide eyed as Ragnor sinks down next to the coffin and lifts a body into his arms.

"Oh my god," I whisper, dread and revulsion crawling over my skin. "That's Sam's mother."

Ragnor is holding a skeleton dressed in a white lace dress.

With nothing but bone and rotting flesh to fill it out, the dress hangs loose. Ragnor strokes the corpse's mangled hair.

I clench my lips together as vomit pools in my belly.

Sam can't look. His eyes are screwed shut and he has turned his face toward Nico. As if he's trying to offer words of comfort, Nico shoves one of the wolves aside and starts whispering to Sam.

If Ragnor cares why Sam attacked him or what's happening between him and Nico, he doesn't show it. He doesn't even seem to register that I'm here. All he can do is stare at the corpse bride in his arms.

When Ragnor is standing up right, Eve turns her back on us and faces the altar. It starts to rain. The sky rumbles as heavy, stinging stripes of water batter the ground and our faces. Clouds obscure the moon. It is almost pitch dark. Then the air starts to quiver. At first, I think I'm seeing lightning again. Except it comes from nowhere. Suspended in mid-air, it crackles and sparks, then grows wider. As if the air directly above the altar is being torn in two, a hole appears. It has jagged edges and curls in on itself.

Fear and nausea pound in my chest; Eve is quite literally ripping open another dimension. Darkness quivers behind the hole. Pure darkness, unlike anything I've ever seen.

A voice fills the air. A voice with no form. As it speaks, terror grips my soul. "Do you have what I need?" it asks.

Ragnor steps forward, still holding his decaying bride. "I do, My King."

"Give it to me."

"If I give you the name of The Phoenix, you will bring back my wife?"

"That was our pact," the voice replies.

Without hesitation, Ragnor answers, "I can do better than a name, My King." He turns and looks at us over his shoulder. A smirk stretches across his face. Perhaps he knew all along. Perhaps he knew Sam was here to betray him, and he let it happen because he knew it would lead to this.

"She is here, The Phoenix. And she brought her fated mates with her." Ragnor spits his words as if they're acid on his tongue.

"Very well," the voice booms.

Ragnor stares down at Elena. He is clutching her tight. As if he's offering a newborn to be baptized, he holds her out in front of him.

"A life for a life." The voice speaks slowly.

"Yes," Ragnor nods. "The Phoenix for Elena."

"No." The voice grows louder. "Dark magick has its own laws, Ragnor. You know this."

"I…" Ragnor stutters. His arms are growing tired. He adjusts his grip on Elena's dead body and shakes his head at the invisible demon he's speaking to. "I don't understand."

"If you want your wife, you must give something of yourself in return." The voice changes. It sounds like it's enjoying Ragnor's torture. "Your blood for her life."

"My blood?" Ragnor stumbles forward. He starts to yell, "What would be the point in that?! I want to be with her! You promised I would be with her. After everything I did for you. Twenty years, I have searched for The Phoenix. Twenty years I have waited—"

As if it's coming from everywhere and nowhere, rattling the walls of the mansion and shaking the ground, the voice explodes with rage. "You did not do it for me. You did it for you!"

Ragnor stumbles backward. He drops Elena and falls to the floor, grappling to pull her back into his arms. "I'm sorry," he pleads. "Just tell me what you want. Please, just tell me."

The voice doesn't answer. Silence echoes around The Hollow. Eve is the one who speaks. Stepping down from her podium, she crouches in front of Ragnor and takes his hands in hers. Her eyes are deathly black. "Your kin, Ragnor. If you want Elena back, you must sacrifice one of your kin. A life for a life. Blood for blood."

A wailing sound fills my ears. I try to shove my hands over them, but I can't move. Hurtling forward, Nico's mother is howling like a wolf. She grabs Ragnor's face in her hands. "You cannot choose Nico," she says. "Not Nico. Not after everything you took from me, Ragnor."

Ragnor stands slowly, seemingly trying to regain his composure as he peels Kayla's hands from his face. He looks down at Elena, and it's obvious what he's thinking; if she comes back, she'll want her baby. She'll want Sam.

Relief rushes over me. Ragnor won't choose Sam. He won't. He can't.

"Do you want to share her?" Kayla snaps, staring up at him from where she cowers on the floor. "Do you want her to love you or Sam? If Sam's here, she'll want him by her side. Is that what *you* want?"

Eve is watching them with glee on her face. "You need to choose, Ragnor," she says, her eyes rolling back in her head. "Time is ticking. Tick-tock, tick-tock."

"Ragnor, you can't choose Nico," Kayla pleads.

I look at Nico. He and Sam are standing now, side-by-side. They join hands.

"Give him Sam, live the rest of your life with Elena, and let me take Nico away. Give me that, Ragnor." Kayla scrambles to her feet and grabs his hand. "You owe me that, at least."

"Tick-tock," Eve cries. "Tick-tock."

"All right!" Ragnor's voice leaves his body in a rush of thunder. "I have chosen." He turns slowly toward Nico and Sam. When his gaze moves from Nico's face, my body doubles over and pain ricochets through me.

"No," I whisper. "No, please, no."

Ragnor doesn't speak Sam's name, just jerks his head at the wolves next to him. As they shove him forward, Sam doesn't resist.

Eve puts her hands on Sam's shoulders. She positions him in front of the altar and the huge glowing tear in the sky. He is facing Ragnor. Kayla falls to her knees. She's crying and clutching her stomach. "Thank you, Ragnor," she yowls. "Thank you."

I am numb. I can't move or breathe or think. Luther is trying to reach for me, but he can't. I feel Kole, and Mack, and Tanner behind me but I can't see them. The crack in the earth is growing. The tear in the sky glows brighter. And Sam isn't fighting. He isn't trying to escape. He's just standing there. Why is he just standing there?

Eve lifts a long silver sword from the altar. Another guttural cry fills the air. This time it's coming from me.

She gestures for Ragnor to take it. He looks into his arms, then steps forward and lays Elena on the ground. Sam is standing stock still. The way he did when Luther and I first met him, when his face was masked, and his body owned by someone else.

I want him to look at me. Why won't he look at me?

Ragnor takes the sword from Eve. He weighs it up and down in his hands. I can't see his face. I have no idea if he looks sorrowful or if he truly doesn't care. As he draws the sword back, Sam's eyes find mine.

I call his name, but his expression doesn't change. He just stares into my eyes. Then he mouths, "I love you," and Ragnor thrusts the sword toward him.

I can't look away. I wait for the blade to pierce Sam's skin. Then something flashes in the corner of my vision. Sam's face disappears. I'm no longer looking at him. I'm looking at Nico.

At the exact moment Nico throws his body in front of Sam's, Ragnor's blade reaches him. With all his weight behind it, the sword enters Nico's stomach and is buried up to the hilt.

Ragnor is still for a moment then staggers back, pulling the blade with him.

Nico wavers on the spot. A puddle of blood stains his shirt. He presses his palms to his stomach. Sam stumbles sideways and takes hold of Nico as he falls.

Kayla starts to scream and tries to rush forward but Ragnor throws his arm around her waist and drags her back.

Sam is cradling Nico in his lap. Tears stream down his face. Nico looks up at him and whispers something. Sam shakes his head, desperately pressing his hands to the wound. Behind them, the tear is growing larger and brighter. I yell for Sam to run. He doesn't look at me. He has Nico's face in his hands, touching their foreheads together. Nico clutches Sam's fingers with his own bloodied hand.

Finally, Sam slides his knees from beneath Nico's head and stands up. Nico's head rolls back. He coughs. Blood trickles from his mouth. The hole behind him grows larger. Eve jumps to one side as it swallows the altar, the skulls, and the coffin. When it reaches Nico, his eyes are already closed. It sucks him in. He disappears in a hiss of bright light.

Sam is shaking. Blood stains his hands and his chest. I need him to run. *Run, Sam, please run.*

Finally, he starts to move.

Ragnor is picking up Elena, shouting, "What happens now?" at the sky.

"Take her to the fountain." Eve sings. "Place her in the water, and The Shadow King will keep his promise." She is shaking her outstretched arms, waving them wildly, cooing and humming and chanting words I don't understand.

Ragnor turns and runs for the fountain. Behind him, the

window to the underworld is still growing. It's swallowing up the earth, following the line of skulls, creating a huge gaping gorge in the ground.

Sam darts around Ragnor. He doesn't look at his mother. His eyes are fixed on mine. My heart lifts. He'll make it. He's fast. He'll make it.

Then suddenly he stops and breaks from my gaze. He looks down. Kayla has hold of him. With one arm around his waist, she hooks the other around his neck, pulls, and throws him to the ground. Her face contorts with anger.

Sam scrambles sideways, barely a foot from the hole that is eating up the earth, but Kayla kicks him hard. He tries to catch hold of her. She kicks him again. He grabs her foot, but she yanks it free, diving sideways.

Sam finds me again. His eyes widen. Then I hear myself scream as the ground below him crumbles. For a second, he grips the edge of the hole. His nails dig into the damp soil. He tries to heave himself out, pulling up tufts of grass, his shoulders bulging with the effort of hanging on. He screams, agony darkening his face. He slips. His fingers drag two deep grooves in the earth as his body disappears into the blackness beneath him.

The last thing I hear before the ground swallows him is, "Nova!"

And then he's gone.

LOVE EMBERS?

If you enjoyed Embers, I would be incredibly grateful if you'd leave a review so that others can discover it too!

As an independent author, reviews are one of the most important tools we have to help spread the word about our books.

Even if it's short, it will be *hugely* appreciated.

You can leave reviews on Amazon, Goodreads, or Storygraph - just search for The Phoenix Prophecy and hit 'leave a review'.

ABOUT CARA

If you love why-choose romance, magic, super-hot mages, and even hotter RH scenes, then we're destined to be friends.

www.caraclare.com

amazon.com/Cara-Clare/e/B09ZQRV4QG
tiktok.com/@caraclareauthor
instagram.com/caraclareauthor

THANK YOU

Thank you for reading Nova by Cara Clare. If you are looking for more books to get lost in please check out our other published titles at;

www.apbeswickpublications.com.
A.P Beswick Publications
Oswaldtwistle Mills Business Centre
Clifton Mill
Pickup Street
Accrington
BB53AP